The bowl of water still stood on the table, and I went and sat in front of it, just as Juniper and Wise Child had done. I could see down through the water to a circular design engraved in the bottom of the bowl. Then something unexpected happened. As I watched the circle, it began to revolve, slowly at first, then quite fast, and it was as if I were being drawn down into it by a powerful force. I suddenly saw a young man's face, his eyes open as if in shock. Then there was a huge house, or what had been a house. It stood blackened and stark, its roof gone, its windows fallen, its walls covered with creepers. This depressing scene suddenly changed. There was light, a hazel tree, a tor lit by the afternoon sun, and an unexpected sense of hope.

I returned to myself with a sort of jolt. There I was, sitting in front of an ordinary bowl of water, and yet it did not seem to be an ordinary bowl at all. . . .

COLMAN

Also by Monica Furlong

WISE CHILD
JUNIPER

COLMAN

· foreword by Karen Cushman ·
MONICA FURLONG

Random House New York

Text copyright © 2004 by the Estate of Monica Furlong.
Foreword copyright © 2004 by Karen Cushman.
Cover art copyright © 2004 by Leo and Diane Dillon.
All rights reserved under International and Pan-American
Copyright Conventions. Published in the United States by
Random House Children's Books, a division of Random House, Inc.,
New York, and simultaneously in Canada by Random House of
Canada Limited, Toronto. Originally published in hardcover by
Random House, Inc., in 2004. First paperback edition February 2005.

www.randomhouse.com/kids

Library of Congress Cataloging-in-Publication Data
Furlong, Monica.
Colman / by Monica Furlong. — 1st ed.   p.   cm.   Sequel to: Wise child.
SUMMARY: After Juniper and her companions find that the Cornwall, England,
castle where she was raised as a princess has been destroyed, they devise a
plan to use magic to oppose the oppression of the evil Meroot and the
Gray Knight and to restore the authority of Prince Brangwyn.
ISBN 0-375-81514-7 (trade)
ISBN 0-375-91514-1 (lib. bdg.)
ISBN 0-375-81515-5 (pbk.)
[1. Magic—Fiction. 2. Witchcraft—Fiction. 3. England—History—Fiction.]
I. Title.   PZ7.F96638Co 2004   [Fic]—dc22 2003019891

Printed in the United States of America
10 9 8 7 6 5 4 3 2

RANDOM HOUSE and colophon are registered trademarks of Random House, Inc.

COLMAN

FOREWORD

Once upon a time, I was in a bookstore, searching for something to read on an airplane flight. It had to be a small paperback, easy to carry, easy to read, and easy to put down and pick up again. I was bored with mysteries, don't like romances, and didn't want anything about death, destruction, or the end of dreams. In the adult section of the store, my selection was limited.

But on a table of children's books was a book with a mysterious and beautiful cover—a richly dressed woman, a wide-eyed child, and what looked like a talking potato. I was intrigued.

Wise Child, the book was called, and its elegant cover was by Leo and Diane Dillon. I bought it and read it before I even left for the airport. Now I had no airplane book, so instead of reading on the flight, I slept, dreaming of the gentle wise woman Juniper, the confused and reluctant Wise Child, Cormac the leper, and Colman, young and brave and devoted to Wise Child. Who could read that book and not yearn for the sweet, simple life of Juniper's house?

That book was my introduction to Monica Furlong. She was a writer of fantasies for young people, and she lived in England. That's all I knew until my friend the Reverend Robbie Cranch, who seizes all opportunities, wrote to Monica all the way in England about her love for *Wise Child*. Monica wrote back, and so began a correspondence that lasted until Monica's final illness.

Monica Furlong was not only a writer of fantasy but also a journalist, broadcaster, poet, travel writer, biographer, and religious rebel. She was born in Kenton, northwest of London, to a family that wanted a boy. She once said she was sorry she hadn't been born early enough to be a suffragette, fighting for the right of women to vote. Dreadfully shy, with a disabling stammer and a fear of the telephone, she nevertheless obtained a job as telephone-answering secretary to a producer for BBC Radio. And her stammer did not prevent her from later success as a journalist, religious broadcaster for the BBC, and outspoken leader of the movement to ordain women in the Anglican Church.

Baptized as a child, she later left the Church only to return after what she called an overwhelming experience of the love of God. Her interest in and devotion to religion led her to write biographies of several religious figures, two books about the successes and decline of the Church of England, and her autobiography, *Bird of Paradise*.

Still, Monica Furlong remains to me the woman who

gave me *Wise Child,* a book so loving and true and, well, wise, that it became an instant classic in my home. In a place that might be Scotland, at a time that might be the Middle Ages, the homeless Wise Child is sent to live with the local wise woman, Juniper. Wise Child slowly grows in wisdom and self-reliance, learning Latin, mathematics, herbal and healing lore, and a bit about the making of magic. When sickness and hunger stalk the village, the local priest accuses Juniper of being a witch, responsible for the village's troubles. Juniper, Wise Child, Cormac, and Colman must run, into an unknown future.

Some church journalists reprimanded Monica for writing about a woman who might be a witch. In a letter to Robbie, Monica wrote, "I think a good deal about witches, because I care a lot about harmony in nature, respecting the environment, and women's proper power. . . . I am a practicing Christian . . . but I feel very unhappy about the Christian treatment of witches, which I believe to have been a particularly virulent form of misogyny." Later she was quoted as saying, "Their [her critics'] claim is that we are out to wipe out God and replace Him with earth goddesses, to destroy the Church and replace it with . . . dancing in sacred groves and celebrating Beltane. . . . The revolution I at least have in mind is a very different one in which the Church might genuinely treat women as equals."

With her gently feminist perspective, Monica Furlong tells in *Wise Child* a spellbinding story, rich in detail, about all the important things in life: good and evil, love and hate, appearance and reality, and loyalty, bigotry, and magic. Many years after I first encountered *Wise Child*, I wrote *Catherine, Called Birdy* and *The Midwife's Apprentice*. I didn't realize until I reread *Wise Child* recently what a debt I owe to its author.

Like all the fans of *Wise Child*, I longed for years for a sequel. But when it came, *Juniper* did not continue the story of Juniper and Wise Child's escape. Instead, it began the story of Juniper from her early life as a princess of Cornwall, long before the events of *Wise Child*. The young Juniper—cranky, stubborn, and pampered—protests when she is sent to learn from Euny, an impoverished wise woman. From Euny, Juniper learns of herbs and magic, love and friendship, and her own growing "powers of the mending sort, the healing sort." When the sorceress Meroot and her husband, the Gray Knight, threaten Cornwall, only Juniper and Euny can save it.

Like everyone else, I've had to wait until now for the continuation of Wise Child's story. This last book of the trilogy is a tale of sea voyages, devastation, courage and fear, and the importance of love and loyalty. Once again, Juniper, Wise Child, Cormac, and Colman struggle to save their land from a powerful evil. What a pleasure lies ahead for you readers about to encounter *Colman*!

The Times (London) once praised *Juniper* for its "strong, resourceful, wise women." Furlong, the paper said, is "a profound and disturbing author who sheds light on our lingering darkness and speaks for tolerance in an intolerant world."

With compassion and commitment, Monica Furlong spent her life searching for truth. Friends remember her as a life-enhancing presence, full of laughter and enthusiasm, passionate, warm, and honest. In truth, she sounds much like Juniper, the warm and wise woman whom we love through her books.

Monica Furlong died of cancer in January 2003. She is survived by a son, a daughter, and numberless fans.

Karen Cushman
April 2003

COLMAN

CHAPTER ONE

Four of us escaped on Finbar's ship after Juniper's trial as a witch—Juniper, Wise Child, Cormac, and me. There had been so much fear for all of us except Finbar, a terrible walk across the island for Juniper and Wise Child, and then suddenly we were all sailing across a peaceful sea, safe at last. It was only a few weeks since Juniper had lived at the white house, had taken care of my cousin Wise Child, and had helped the people of the village with remedies for their sicknesses and accidents. Then came the accusation of black magic, with the sequel of torture and possible death, and Juniper, who had been arrested and imprisoned, had only just escaped in time.

And now there the five of us were on the ship, along with Finbar's men. It was a beautiful evening. Juniper and Wise Child sat in the stern of the boat watching the sunset and recovering from their ordeal, Wise Child small and dark, Juniper with her arm around her. Juniper's long black hair blew wildly about until she put her shawl over it to tame it. Cormac stood staring over the stern with his scarred, damaged face, seeing the island grow smaller and smaller. I guess he had few regrets for the place where he had known great unhappiness. Me, although I felt bad about leaving Mam and my brothers and sisters without saying goodbye, I was very glad to get away from Dad and his belt and to have started an adventure with the people I loved best, not counting my family.

It was terribly exciting to be on a ship like Finbar's. It had sails, something I had never seen before. The island boats were small and light and made out of wicker and hide, whereas Finbar's boat, like the *birlinns* on which I had very occasionally traveled to the mainland with my father, was made out of wood. And now, with the wind behind us, we had begun to move rapidly and would sail for distances I had barely dreamed of. Already we had passed islands of which I did not even know the names.

I followed Finbar about, listening to him giving orders and imagining myself as captain of a ship. Soon Finbar suggested chores I could do like a proper sailor. One of the men showed me how to coil a rope, and Cully, the ship's cook, got me peeling vegetables in the galley.

That first night was a joyful one. Finbar broached some wine, and even Wise Child and I were given a generous amount with a splash of water. It was too soon to start asking any of the difficult questions about where we would go and what we would do. We were all just glad to be together and to be safe.

I did notice that Wise Child seemed a little shy of Finbar. Although he was her dad, he had been at sea for several years, and she had looked forward to his return for so long. I think she was surprised to find that he seemed like a stranger to her. Perhaps his sheer size was intimidating. Finbar was a very tall man with a beard and strong, handsome features. He had black hair and brilliant blue eyes, just like her own, along with wonderful pale skin.

We enjoyed our feast—we were all really hungry—and then Finbar found beds for all of us. He turned out of his bunk and put Juniper in it. Wise Child he put in a little made-up bed on the floor. He slung hammocks for himself and for Cormac and me on the deck. I did not go to sleep for hours—it seemed a pity to waste my excitement in sleep. I loved watching the movement of the stars overhead and feeling the gentle movement of the ship.

I fell asleep at last and slept well, but was awakened in the early morning by shouting. A strong wind was blowing, and the sea had become much rougher. The sailors were clambering up the mast and along the yardarm, pulling in sails and tying them into place.

I hastily did up my trousers and folded my hammock, wanting to be part of it all. We were passing through a channel with land on both sides.

"That's Ireland!" one of the sailors shouted to me, pointing to starboard. "They call this the North Channel!"

Before I could offer my services as a sailor, Finbar

ordered me down to the galley. Cully was already at work gutting some fish, and I helped him clean up afterward.

"Fancy a bit of bacon, boy?" he asked when we had finished.

I nodded.

"The sea hasn't put you off your breakfast, then?"

I thought about it. No, my stomach felt fine.

"I'd like your help. There's a lot to do on a ship on a morning like this, and it's important not to get in the men's way."

It occurred to me later that Finbar had asked him to tell me this in a way that did not hurt my feelings.

"Have you washed?" he then surprised me by asking.

I shook my head.

"Must keep clean on a ship, 'specially when you're a cook." He nodded to a flagon of water in the corner with a cloth beside it, and under his eye I washed my face and hands. I had not realized sailors were so fussy. Then I started chopping onions until the tears ran down my face. I had just started on a mound of cabbage when a sailor appeared at the door.

"Cap'n sends his compliments and would like to talk to you, sir," he said to me. "He's at the wheel."

I was so overcome at being called "sir" that I just mumbled, "All right," but Cully prompted me quietly: "Aye, aye." I duly echoed him, then followed the sailor above deck.

Finbar made a fine figure at the wheel and for a few moments did not speak to me. Finbar, I was to learn, was a man of long silences.

"We're having a council of war tonight, Colman," he said at last. "All of us, to decide where to go, what to do. But I wanted to talk to you first.

"It seems bad luck that you have got caught up in all this and dragged away from your family. I dare not let you go back, however. They would certainly suspect you were involved in the escape because of your friendship with Wise Child."

I nodded. If I went back, there would be endless questions, and my dad would do his best to beat the truth out of me. I was much more frightened of him than I was of Cormac's brother, Fillan, the priest who, during the time of famine and the smallpox epidemic, had roused the people against Juniper. There was little hardship for me in going on a voyage with my favorite people.

The effort of explaining all this felt too great. I grinned instead and said, "I don't mind!"

Finbar looked at me in a searching way with eyes that were so much like Wise Child's. Then he shook his head slightly and laughed. "So be it!"

It was not till I saw Wise Child and Juniper in Finbar's cabin that evening that I realized that though they had escaped, the ordeal was not over for them. The previous night they had seemed calm, serene. Tonight, however,

Juniper looked pale and drawn, entirely unlike her usual rosy self. There were shadows under her eyes, and she kept propping up her head. with her hand as if she was too exhausted to hold it upright.

Wise Child had been seasick in the course of the day. Now she lay on Finbar's bunk, white and indifferent, with closed eyes. I don't think at that moment she cared very much what became of her.

"I know this is not a good time for you, but we need to make some plans," Finbar began. "Obviously, it may be months, or even years, before you can return to the white house."

"If ever," put in Juniper quietly.

"So that we need to think what to do next," Finbar continued. "Cormac has an idea that he has put to me."

Finbar nodded at our friend, and we all leaned in close to listen. Until Juniper had healed him, Cormac had been afflicted by leprosy. Though his sores had closed, his face, with its mutilated nose and twisted mouth, would be forever scarred. Cormac's speech was never easy to understand, but that night his meaning came across quite clearly.

"We are near Ireland now and will be for some hours," he said. "Just before the southeastern tip there is a big harbor, an estuary, into which the river Slaney opens. If you follow the Slaney for an hour or so, you come to a small harbor for the village of Ennis. It is there that my aunt and uncle live, and where I grew up after my mother died. My aunt and uncle have a large farm. I am sure we could use one of the barns for a few weeks while we make our future plans. Juniper and Wise Child need a place where they can rest and be looked after for a bit, and my aunt would understand that."

Cormac looked tenderly at Juniper as he said this, and his badly scarred face looked more like that of the man he must once have been.

"I like the idea," said Finbar. "We could be there tomorrow." He looked questioningly at Juniper, and suddenly I realized all that Juniper had lost and perhaps would never see again—her beautiful white house on the mountain, her land, her herbs, and her animals.

"What do you think?" Finbar said to Juniper.

"I like Cormac's idea," she said, "as long as our stay is a brief one. It may be foolish of me, but I cannot quite give up the idea that when Fillan cannot find me and Wise Child on the island and realizes that Cormac has disappeared, too, it might just occur to him that somehow we have got across the sea to Ennis. Probably that is entirely fanciful, but that is my fear."

"It's not entirely a fancy," Finbar put in. "The *Holy Trinity* apart, you might have hired a boat from someone, and they may think of that."

"I think it will take him a while to get round to that possibility, even if he cares enough to pursue me," said Juniper. "In the long term, however, I can see only one solution, which is that we go to Cornwall. My father is *regulus* there, as you know, and will give us a piece of land if I ask him, perhaps build us a house."

We always tended to forget it, but Juniper was, of course, a princess, the daughter of King Mark, the *regulus* of Cornwall.

"I thought you might say that, and I think that should be our goal," said Finbar. "For the time being, however, I favor Cormac's idea."

He looked kindly at Juniper. I knew from my mother's gossip that he and Juniper had been sweethearts many years earlier, before Wise Child's mother had lured him away.

"Might it not be awkward for you, Cormac?" Juniper asked. "Presumably your aunt would also regard Fillan as kin."

"Fillan left home as a lad of twelve to pursue his studies with the monks," said Cormac, "and has never been back. They never liked him much, nor he them. He's almost forgotten there. I don't think that will be a problem." He paused. "However, some said that Aunt Brigid loved me more than her own son. That was one of the reasons I left. Columb became jealous, and I did not want to cause trouble. If there are any objections, they will come from him."

"I think we should try it," said Finbar. "I do not think Wise Child and Juniper should have to spend much longer at sea. Are we agreed?"

There was a murmur of assent.

"Wise Child? Is there anything you want to say?" Finbar asked.

My cousin groaned. "I just want to get off the boat," she said.

"I sympathize," said Finbar briskly, not as if he sympathized much at all. I guess he had seen a good deal of seasickness in his years at sea.

"Colman?"

Somehow, I could not do anything except smile. I would go anywhere with these people. Earlier that day the wind had dropped a bit, and Finbar had let me take the wheel for a spell. "He's as good as a cabin boy!" one of the sailors had said, and although I knew he was trying to be nice, I was pleased. I was loving the voyage.

The next day, as the light was waning, we sailed up the estuary of the Slaney. Cormac stood at the wheel beside Finbar, telling him the vagaries of the river, and soon we arrived at the harbor of Ennis. There was no one around as we anchored, lowered the dinghy, and rowed across to shore.

"I'll go on ahead," said Cormac after we had landed, "and talk to my aunt and uncle."

I thought he seemed suddenly nervous, and it occurred to me that the sight of him might be a shock to his relatives. Cormac had become a leper only after leaving Ireland and rather than return home had made his way to Fillan, hoping for help and sanctuary. But Fillan had turned

Cormac away, believing his illness to be the result of his sins. Now Cormac's sores were healed, but it was still a shock for anyone to see him for the first time. I wondered how his aunt would bear it.

As we waited by the harbor, a wave of gloom spread across us. Somehow, since Cormac had suggested the idea, we had seized upon Ennis as a haven in our trouble, and now the fear crept in that we might not be wanted. It was cold, and Juniper and Wise Child were shivering, huddled together for warmth. I had an impression that Juniper had a touch of fever—her cheeks looked hot, and her eyes were too big.

"It can't be an easy story to tell," Finbar murmured at one point, looking in the direction where Cormac had disappeared.

Eventually, after it had grown quite dark, we saw the light of torches in the distance and heard the sound of cheerful voices. Cormac called out to us, and Finbar went forward. We heard him talking to Cormac's companions. Then the group approached, and we could see them clearly in the torchlight—an elderly man and woman with kindly expressions and a younger couple. Several servants held the torches.

"This is my aunt Brigid," said Cormac, introducing the older woman, "and this my uncle Brendan."

I noticed tears in the eyes of Cormac's aunt. "Imagine my joy," she said, with Cormac translating for us, "at seeing this one again. I thought I had lost him for good. It is a glorious day for us to have him back!"

I noticed the younger couple exchange glances, and I doubted they were as pleased as their parents to see their cousin again.

Cormac's aunt turned to Juniper. "But it's sorry I am to hear you are not well," she said. "You and the little girl. I have told the servants to make up beds for you in the house. If the men don't mind the barn, there is plenty of hay there, and we will give you some blankets." She held out her arms to Juniper, embraced her for a moment, and then started walking back with her in the direction of the house with an arm around her. It seemed to me that Juniper needed her support, and I wondered how Cormac had explained what ailed her.

That first night the hospitality was all that we could have asked for. The servants were busy making a meal when we arrived at the house. Juniper and Wise Child were carried off and put to bed. The rest of us were shown the barn, where there was plenty of room for us to sleep among the piles of soft hay. Then we went back to the house for a huge meal.

Soon after it was over I felt overcome by sleep and crept away to the barn. My dreams were broken by the men laughing and telling stories, and once I heard Finbar's voice raised in song.

❁   ❁   ❁

Wise Child recovered more quickly than Juniper, at least as
far as physical well-being was concerned; she was soon out
of bed. As if her suffering had changed her, or perhaps it
was only that my perception had changed, she suddenly
seemed taller, more grown-up, not a little girl anymore. I
also noticed that she seemed unusually bad-tempered. I
supposed she missed the security and comfort of the white
house and perhaps of having Juniper all to herself.

Once, I overheard a conversation between her and
Juniper. I was sitting on the doorstep of the farm whittling
a boat with a knife Cormac's uncle had given me and did
not at first pay any attention.

"Do you think you are cross with Finbar for having
stayed away so long?" I suddenly heard Juniper say quite
clearly.

"Why should I be?" said Wise Child, sounding very
cross indeed.

"Because he left you all alone with no one to look
after you and did not come back for several years."

"I *did* have someone to look after me—my grannie.
And then I had you."

"Yes, but he knew that your grannie was very old, and
he was not to know that I would take you in."

Wise Child said nothing, and I could imagine the
obstinate expression on her face. Juniper went on just as if
she had spoken.

"You know, it might be easier for you both if you

said that to him—that you felt he abandoned you. Then you could be close again like you used to be."

Wise Child must have felt very upset because she suddenly shouted, "It's not your business!" and stormed out.

It seemed too late then to announce my presence.

After about a week of struggling with fever, during which Cormac's aunt nursed her, Juniper spent less time in bed. She still looked very thin and tired, but she had begun to eat again and to take short walks around the farm.

One day, when we had been at the farm for about three weeks, she said she thought Wise Child and I should do some lessons. She set up a table and chairs in the barn, managed to borrow some wax tablets and styluses from the village, and we spent the morning working. This was difficult for me because Wise Child was so much cleverer than me. It made me feel miserable.

Juniper came and sat on the well one afternoon when I was drawing water and said she wanted to talk to me about lessons. I thought she was going to tell me that it was hopeless trying to teach me, and I went red and kicked the bricks at the base of the well. It is awful to feel more stupid than other people.

"I can't help it," I mumbled before she could say anything. "I'm just no good at it. I feel a real fool."

"I never heard such nonsense," Juniper amazed me by saying. "Of course, you have not had the teaching Wise Child has had, and nobody knows what they have not been taught. But what I wanted to tell you was that I have never seen anybody learn more quickly than you do. You really work at it, whether you can do it or not, and that is the real secret. So for heaven's sake, don't start getting discouraged!

"I want to make some suggestions, though," she continued. "I know you are very interested in sailing. I am going to ask Finbar to teach you sailors' lore in the mornings, when Wise Child and I are busy with lessons. Then you can share lessons with Wise Child—history and geography and stories. You and I will work by ourselves at writing and reading and languages so that you won't feel a fool. I promise that you will do just as well as Wise Child with a bit more help."

I soon realized, however, that Wise Child did not like it much when Juniper gave me lessons by myself. She would think of reasons to interrupt and become defiant with Juniper in a way I had never noticed before. I also began to realize that since we had left the island, there had been no talk of magic. Sometimes I wondered if I had made up the whole idea of Juniper training Wise Child to be a *doran,* a wise person like herself who used magic to heal the world.

One afternoon I entered the barn, and it was so still and silent that I thought it was empty. Then I noticed Juniper sitting at the table with a large bowl of water in front of her.

"What are you—" I began, but Juniper said, "Shh!" I

sat down as quietly as I could. Juniper sat in total concentration for a while, staring into the water, and then, as if that had finished, shook herself and turned to me.

"Colman, do you think you could find Wise Child?" she asked.

Grumbling as she did when asked to do almost anything now, Wise Child came to the barn.

"I want you to use the water," Juniper said. "You know how."

A look of fury crossed Wise Child's face. She moved slowly and unwillingly to the table and sat down. I know I should have gone away, but I was fascinated to see what would happen.

For the next few minutes Wise Child sat there, sighing at intervals. Finally Juniper said, quite sharply, "It's no good sighing and wanting to be somewhere else, as you know very well. You need to give yourself up to it."

Wise Child continued to fidget until Juniper said, "Well, I'll leave you to it for a bit. Come, Colman, we'll go for a little walk."

When we came back, Wise Child was sitting outside by the well, swinging a foot in obvious exasperation.

"I couldn't see anything," she called out as soon as we came in earshot.

"I'm sorry to hear it," said Juniper. "I needed your eyes."

I was not sure whether they wanted to go on discussing

it, so, trying to be tactful, I wandered back inside the barn. The bowl of water still stood on the table, and I went and sat in front of it, just as Juniper and Wise Child had done. Juniper had told me that what they had been doing was called scrying. I knew that I did not have the knack that Juniper and Wise Child did of seeing and hearing things other people could not see and hear and of sometimes knowing things about the future. It was annoying when Wise Child had used to go on and on about it, but the truth was I did not really want to be able to do it. I thought it was all a bit creepy, and life was quite interesting enough as it was. But nevertheless, because I was curious, I sat down in front of the bowl of water.

There was nothing to see in its shadowy depths, with highlights reflecting the sunlight that came into the barn through the doorway. Its surface was occasionally ruffled by drafts. I could see down through the water to a circular design engraved in the bottom of the bowl. Then something unexpected happened. As I watched the circle, it began to revolve, slowly at first, then quite fast, and it was as if I were being drawn down into it by a powerful force. I suddenly saw a young man's face, his eyes open as if in shock. Then there was a huge house, or what had been a house. It stood blackened and stark, its roof gone, its windows fallen, its walls covered with creepers. This depressing scene suddenly changed. There was light, a hazel tree, a tor lit by the afternoon sun, and an unexpected sense of hope.

I returned to myself with a sort of jolt. There I was, sitting in front of an ordinary bowl of water, and yet it did not seem to be an ordinary bowl at all. I did not know what to make of it and crept away to my bed in the hay to think it out. Was this what Juniper had wanted Wise Child to do? What had Juniper herself seen? Regardless, I felt too shy to discuss it with either of them.

I liked life on the farm. It was a prosperous place, and there was lots to eat, more than I had ever been used to at home. I always felt slightly ashamed of the way we did not have enough food at home, though it was nobody's fault. I think I felt this way because it embarrassed other people if they knew about it. But not being hungry most of the time did make life more enjoyable.

I loved Cormac's aunt and uncle, who piled food on my plate and generally spoiled me, always wanting to know what I had been doing. We talked with some difficulty. There were lots of words in our languages that were the same, but we got into some terrible muddles trying to understand one another, which made us laugh a lot.

We had some wonderful times together. Uncle Brendan asked me one day if I liked to fish, which, of course, I did, though I had never had a proper rod. He lent me one, and the two of us went on trips up the Slaney and caught some trout. Then Cormac, who like so many Irishmen was a great horseman, asked if Wise Child and I wanted to ride, and he borrowed some ponies small enough for us to use. We both enjoyed riding, following Cormac's instructions about how to sit and how to control our mounts.

During this time I began to notice that Wise Child and I no longer had the close conversations we'd used to have, in which we confided in each other about the details of our lives. Of course, in a way we had no need to, since we lived in and around the farm together. Still, I could not get away from the feeling that Wise Child was angry with me as well as with Juniper and Finbar. This made me sad because I loved Wise Child and felt she was not happy.

Spring was coming slowly—already it was growing dark later, though the nights were cold—and I found myself hoping that we might be allowed to stay at the farm until summer had come.

One night, however, I was slipping over to the farmhouse to toast my feet by the fire as Aunt Brigid liked me to do when I heard from outside the door the sound of two voices quarreling. At once I recognized Columb and Cormac, though they were talking too fast in Irish for me to understand fully what they said. All I knew for sure was that Columb was angry.

Cormac then said something I partly understood, something about staying till the weather improved, and this time I more or less got the drift of Columb's words.

"You must greet the spring elsewhere with your witch and her child," he said. "That is, unless you want me to send word to Fillan. You have outstayed your welcome."

I went back to the barn horrified at what I had heard. Cormac must have passed this information on to Finbar, because the following day he called a meeting. He began by making the suggestion that it was time for us to move on to Cornwall—he said no word of Columb's threats. There was a long silence after he had spoken. I imagine he expected Juniper and Wise Child to protest.

"Juniper?" he said at last.

"I am all in favor of the move," she said. "I was about to suggest it myself."

I could see by the look on Finbar's face that he was astonished. "Why?" he said. "Aren't you happy here?"

"Oh yes," said Juniper, "and grateful for all the wonderful hospitality. I shall always be grateful to your aunt, Cormac. She is the kindest of women. It is just that I feel it is time to go to Cornwall, where I fear that all is not well."

Finbar looked surprised again. However much those of us close to Juniper thought we knew her, she could always take us unawares.

"Why?"

"I just know it," said Juniper simply. "Now that we are all stronger again, it is time to see for ourselves. The sooner the better, in my view."

CHAPTER TWO

When we left Ennis, there was none of the sense of joy
there had been at the beginning of our journey. Juniper
seemed full of unspoken forebodings about what awaited
us, and Cormac was distressed by the tears of his aunt, who
could not understand why we would not stay longer.

Wise Child could see no further than her dread of
feeling seasick. She took some persuading that it was necessary to cross the sea at all to get to Cornwall.

"I'm ashamed of you," said Juniper. "After all my
teaching!" and she promptly drew her a map of England
and Ireland.

"Oh, I know all *that*!" said Wise Child in her best
dismissive style. She never seemed to feel shame at being
unreasonable.

"Well, then. At least you can see it's not very far."

Although Cornwall itself was quite close, we were
going to approach from the south, which meant sailing
round the tip of Cornwall and then along the coast.

"I suppose we could travel overland," Finbar said to

Juniper, "but I know there are brigands in that country, and to sail straight to your father's kingdom seems a safer bet."

Juniper considered this. "I would rather sail round to the south. There are a number of harbors along that coast, and we can leave the ship there while we explore. We'll get a feel of what is happening and return to the ship if we need to."

"You feel something bad has happened?"

"*Something* has happened, but how bad it is I don't know. When I am not properly well, I cannot see as clearly as at other times."

Finbar did not waste energy trying to cheer her up or saying that it might not be as bad as she feared. He nodded and said calmly, "Well, we'll go and see for ourselves." They smiled at each other with the ease of old friends.

Contrary to Wise Child's fears, this time the sea was as calm as a millpond, and she gradually realized that she felt perfectly well. This put her in a good mood, or as good a mood as she seemed capable of these days.

"It will be exciting to see Cornwall," I said. We stood on deck watching the seabirds, of which there were many, and watching for seals, which made us laugh because they looked so uncannily human as they held their heads out of the water and stared curiously at the ship.

"I suppose so," she said drearily. "Everything's spoiled anyway."

"You mean because you can't live in Juniper's house anymore?"

"Well, that. And other things."

"You've got Finbar back, anyway. You were longing to see him again."

"It's not the same," Wise Child said. "He was away too long."

"Perhaps it just takes time to get used to him again," I said. "He's nice. He doesn't scare me like my dad does. And there are other good things, aren't there? What about becoming a *doran*? Do you still think about that?"

"I think that's all finished," Wise Child said sharply.

"How can that be?"

"I've lost the gift," she said.

I was so surprised that I was silent, and she went on, "I just can't do it anymore."

"I don't believe it!" I said. "I don't believe people lose their gifts, not unless they do something terribly wrong. Perhaps you've just mislaid it for a bit. What does Juniper think?"

"We don't discuss it," Wise Child said. "Anyway, being a *doran* is a horribly dangerous thing to be. Look at what they tried to do to Juniper. They'd have killed her, no question, if we had not got away."

I could not think of anything encouraging to reply to this. The hatred that Fillan and the others had shown Juniper had been very frightening. All the love and kindness

24

she had shown to the villagers over the years had been forgotten. They'd needed to believe that it was she who had brought the smallpox, or rather they'd needed someone to blame and she was the safest person to pick.

I thought of telling Wise Child that I myself had seen something in the water on the day of the scrying, but I suspected it would make her cross, since she had failed to do so. And then again maybe I had not really seen anything. I was not at all sure. So I said nothing.

Juniper, though still not her old self again, seemed to move more lightly now and appeared more cheerful. As we neared Cornwall, she waited eagerly in the prow of the ship to see her native land. There was a bitter wind blowing, but it was a sunny day, which made the sea look extraordinarily blue, and the coast stood out boldly against the sky. As we got nearer, we could see the great cliffs and the seabirds nesting among them, and beyond them forests and low hills. We rounded the foot of Cornwall and began our journey up the coast on the other side. It was lovely country, rocky and wild, and as far as we could see, empty of human habitation.

Before half a day had passed, we sailed into a narrow break in the rocky walls, which Juniper pointed out to Finbar. Almost immediately this opened out into a natural harbor that was deep enough for Finbar's ship. There, Finbar told us, we would leave his men to look after the ship, and some of us would go ashore to explore. I think he

25

thought of leaving Juniper and Wise Child and me behind while he and Cormac went off to get a feel of the country. Juniper would have none of that.

"We must go together," she said. "We have done no wrong to these people, and I speak their language much better than you do. There is no reason that they should not welcome us."

There was no argument about where we wanted to go. We would head for the Wooden Palace of Castle Dore, where Juniper had spent her childhood. It was, said Juniper, about a day's walk from where we had left the ship. We each carried a little food and water, and a drink fermented from oats that the sailors had given us, but we assumed we would be able to buy more food from farms along the way. Finbar, I noticed, strapped on a sword and had a knife at his belt. Cormac also took a dagger.

Juniper seemed very confident of how to get to Castle Dore, though the forests and paths all looked alike to me. Some of her doubt and fear about what awaited us had infected the rest of us, and we walked in a somber mood— she and Finbar, Cormac and myself, and Wise Child lagging behind and grumbling a good deal. From time to time I noticed Juniper's eyes resting on her thoughtfully.

That night we found what might have been a shepherd's hut out in the fields and slept in it. It turned colder and none of us slept well, though Wise Child and I curled up together and the others lay in a row where there was just enough room for grown-up people to lie full-length. We emerged into a misty dawn, glad to move our cold, cramped limbs and to drink the fermented liquid the sailors had given us, which warmed our bodies. We ate our bread and cheese and started walking again in silence, perhaps feeling some reluctance to reach the end of our journey. What would we learn by nightfall?

"It must be about here that my father's kingdom begins," Juniper said at one point. "We have been walking through what are called the Outlands. The territory he rules stretches from around here to the Northland. The Outlands are the rough country in between. We must be about four hours from the Wooden Palace."

It was early afternoon before we saw any people. We saw a boy sitting on a rock in a clearing with a flock of goats.

Juniper called to him in her own language, and the boy raised his head, startled. He was obviously not expecting to see anyone and was probably unaccustomed to strangers. He was thin and ragged and had the look of hunger on his face that I remembered so well in myself and other children in the village. Juniper spoke to him again, and a look both cunning and frightened crossed his face. He dropped his head and mumbled something.

Juniper turned to Finbar, deeply distressed. "He says the Wooden Palace is deserted!" she said. When she asked the boy why, he shook his head and refused to answer.

"We *must* get there as soon as possible," Juniper said insistently. "Anything may have happened—disease, war. . . ."

Juniper thought for a moment, then said, "There's a place near here where you can see Castle Dore from a long way away. It's on a hill behind the harbor. I think we should make for that."

With a little more walking, we reached the hill Juniper had described. As we climbed to the top, the rays of the dying sun lit up a building in the distance so that it looked as if it were on fire. It was a magnificent house—or it had been once. We could clearly see that its roof was gone and its windows were black, gaping holes.

Suddenly I had the overwhelming feeling that I had seen this place before. But where? Then I knew. It was in the water of the bowl at Aunt Brigid's farm. There before us was the roofless building, the blackened walls, the look of utter desolation.

"It's the same!" I burst out.

Juniper tore her eyes away from the castle to look at me. "What do you mean?"

"I saw it before but didn't know it meant anything. I didn't know I could see things."

"Where? Where did you see it?" Juniper asked.

"In the bowl."

"The scrying bowl?" Even in her distress about Castle Dore, I could see Juniper registering this information about me. Behind Juniper, Wise Child scowled. I had done what she could not, and I knew that she was jealous.

"I didn't mean to," I said awkwardly. "I just looked in the water, and I saw it—the Wooden Palace."

"Did you see anything else?" Juniper wanted to know. "This may be very important, Colman."

I tried to remember what I had seen. "A young man's face . . . ," I told her hesitantly.

"How old was he?"

"About eighteen."

Juniper looked at Finbar. "The age of my little brother, Brangwyn," she said. She turned back to me. "What was his expression?"

"Shocked," I said. "Not frightened, but shocked."

"Thank you," Juniper said quietly. Without another word, she turned and started down the hill.

We walked silently on toward the Wooden Palace. When we were still some distance from it, we passed a gibbet set on a big patch of green grass where, Juniper told us, in her youth people danced in the joy of maying. There was a body hanging on the gibbet. It was not quite a skeleton, and a small flock of birds that had been picking at it flew away at our approach. In the gathering dusk it was a horrible sight.

Soon we were near enough to see the Wooden Palace clearly. I had heard Juniper tell Wise Child stories about her childhood there, and I could see, as we got closer, how big and impressive it had been. Even broken and blackened, it had a somber dignity that came from its fine position. It was set off by the open space around it, and it was surrounded by a huge fortification of grassy ramps and ditches. As we got closer, we could see that it had suffered terrible damage. Some of it was blackened by fire; other parts had been torn away, probably deliberately destroyed by battering rams or men with hammers. Tears ran freely down Juniper's face, and I was glad to see Wise Child fall into step beside her and gently put her hand into hers. Juniper grasped it and squeezed. Finbar, too, who had been a page at the palace, looked set and grim.

It took us a long time to reach the palace, although it had looked near. Juniper led us through the maze of paths toward its entrance. No sentry challenged us; the place appeared to be deserted. One of the great doors of the entrance was gone. The other, a mass of charred wood, hung from one hinge.

We went through a passage into a modest-sized room. It was a sort of anteroom, Juniper explained, where people waited until King Mark was ready to see them. Beyond that was the "king's room," a place where he met councillors and others in private, and beyond that again the council room. This was huge, with a throne at the far end and a circular table in the middle where the *regulus* had sat with his councillors. There were blackened stains on the walls where it looked as if arms had once hung, but these had all gone. I knew from Juniper's face that she was picturing her father sitting on the throne.

We moved out of the council room into the great dining hall. There was a dais at one end where the *regulus* and his family had dined, and a big fireplace in the center with a broken cauldron lying on its side. There were a number of long tables, some charred, some overturned, some broken, as if an army had come upon the king and his knights as they sat at dinner.

A small door at the end of the dining hall led out into a courtyard. To the right, Juniper indicated, was what was left of the apartments of her family. To the left were a number of smaller buildings. Suddenly, from a low building some distance away, we noticed a flicker of light, the first suggestion of human presence that we had seen at Castle Dore.

Juniper at once made a motion toward it.

"Be careful!" Finbar warned. "Let me go first."

"We will go together," said Juniper.

We quietly approached the building—the old bakehouse, Juniper told us—from which firelight continued to flicker. Finbar was in the lead, with Juniper close beside him. Wise Child, Cormac, and I followed a few steps behind. It was cold, and I shivered a little, though whether it was really from the cold I couldn't be sure.

As we drew nearer, I thought I could hear quiet conversation. Juniper called out a gentle greeting in the

31

language of her people, while Finbar clutched the hilt of his sword. Silence fell within, and then, between the fire and the doorway, we could see the outline of a big man.

"Who is it?" he called roughly, and he spoke backward over his shoulder to someone out of sight.

"Two friends," Juniper answered back, and she and Finbar moved nearer. The man came out with a cudgel in his hand, which caused Finbar to draw his sword, and the three eyed one another in the gloaming.

"Lyon!" said Juniper suddenly.

"Who's that?" the man asked.

"Someone who used to know you well. King Mark's daughter, Ninnoc."

The man peered through the dusk.

"How do I know you are Ninnoc?" he asked suspiciously.

"You were King Mark's armorer, and when I was little, you made me a tiny suit of armor once, of which I was very proud. You were married to Merrion, the best dancer in the whole court, and you had five children, all of whom could sing. When I left, your son Lyonel was training as an armorer."

"Little Ninnoc!" Lyon exclaimed with genuine feeling. He lowered his cudgel and stepped forward. On his face was an expression of wonder. "It *is* you. Forgive me for my greeting, but we have to be careful. What are you doing here? Let me look at you—still beautiful. Merrion, come and look here. It is Princess Ninnoc!"

Through the doorway stepped a woman who was bent with sickness, her long gray hair falling loosely about her face. Juniper later told me that Merrion had once been the gayest girl at court.

Juniper held out her arms, and she and Merrion embraced, both of them crying a little.

"And look, Merrion!" Lyon continued. "Here is Finbar. Do you remember that handsome page boy of King Mark's who used to dance with you sometimes? God, but I was jealous of him!"

Merrion curtsied to Finbar.

"Will you sit," said Lyon, "and perhaps share a bowl of soup with us? God knows how you ended up here, but we are delighted to see you. More than you can know!"

Juniper explained about Wise Child, Cormac, and me and gestured for us to join them. We came blinking into the light, and Lyon led us all into the old bakehouse and showed us where to sit on the floor on some old pieces of carpet with a few worn cushions upon it. Merrion at once started ladling soup into chipped earthen bowls, and I was delighted to see it and smell the spring sorrel.

By common consent we did not start on explanations until everyone had drunk their bowl of soup. This, with some rough bread, was clearly the whole supper Lyon and Merrion had been hoping to enjoy, and I wondered whether we had eaten food intended for the next day as well. Juniper, whom I knew to be hungry, firmly refused another bowl of soup, and the rest of us followed her example.

"We heard that you lived away up in the north," Lyon said to Juniper at last. "We never thought to see you again. It's glad I am for it. The only good thing that has happened these last two years."

"I came," Juniper said carefully, "in order to see my father at his court and ask for refuge. I knew, by a sort of rumor, that things were not well here, but I knew no details. Please, please, tell me as carefully as you can what has happened. Don't spare me—I want to know everything."

"Princess . . . ," Lyon began. Lyon was a huge man with broad shoulders, and it was not difficult to imagine him beating armor on an anvil, but as he tried to speak, his voice broke, and he sounded almost as if he might cry.

"Princess," he said again. "King Mark and Queen Erlain . . . they are both dead."

Juniper closed her eyes. While it must have hurt her to hear it said, I somehow think she was not surprised. After a moment she said, "What happened here, Lyon? Where is my brother?"

Lyon picked up a bowl and began fiddling with it, as if needing something to hold on to. "It was two years ago that the horror came to us," he began. "Prince Brangwyn was sixteen at the time, not old enough to be crowned *regulus* but studying the arts of war and of counseling. He was a promising lad, and we all thought the world of him. He was going to be crowned on his eighteenth birthday. He had been a merry boy, always one for a tease or a game, and many a time your father rebuked him and told him to study, and he would shrug his shoulders and laugh. And, saving your father's wishes, people rather liked it that he was a naughty boy. Now, I think, we are glad that he laughed when he could."

He glanced across at Merrion as if for reassurance or verification, and she nodded sadly.

"He was fifteen when King Mark died," Lyon went on, "and it was as if all at once he took on his father's mantle. In fact, the councillors used to beg him not to be so serious, but he would say, 'I am to be *regulus* soon, and I must be worthy of my father.'"

"What did my father die of?" Juniper asked painfully.

"It was very strange. He had seemed in perfect health all winter, and then suddenly, in a week or two, he sickened and died."

I could see Juniper storing this knowledge away to think about later.

"And my mother?"

"She had died several years before. There was an epidemic at the castle—indeed, in the whole district—a sickness with rashes and swellings, and she was one of the victims. We loved Erlain. A great lady, we always thought her. And your father was heartbroken for her, which perhaps was why he was ripe to die. When he did, the councillors began to prepare Prince Brangwyn for kingship."

Lyon's voice suddenly grew rough. "Meroot and the Gray Knight of Caerleon came on a visit, officially to pay their condolences to Brangwyn. Less than two months later their army arrived and occupied the kingdom."

"Meroot!" Juniper exclaimed.

Finbar's eyes flashed with anger. "I guess she finally got what she wanted," he said fiercely.

I looked questioningly at Juniper, and she explained, "Meroot is my aunt—my father's sister. She is also a sorceress. For as long as I have known her, she has coveted Mark's throne. When I was a girl, Finbar and I helped stop her and her husband, the Gray Knight, who is also a sorcerer, from seizing it."

Finbar's face was grim. "What happened?" he asked Lyon.

"They attacked Castle Dore with hatchets, hammers, and rams, and finally they set fire to it," Lyon said. "However long I live I never want to see as terrible a sight as that again. People saw the flames miles away. They forced Brangwyn to watch the palace being destroyed, and then they took him away with them, back to Caerleon."

"And is he . . . dead?" I could feel Juniper hesitating over the hard word.

"By no means. He is much more useful to them alive. They pretend that he still rules this country, though he is not allowed out of Caerleon and we never see him. But they use him to turn us all into his slaves. We have to send tremendous tithes of corn and cattle to Caerleon, which means that we have almost nothing to eat ourselves. If we disobey the Gray Knight in even the smallest particulars, not only does he punish us severely but he threatens to kill Brangwyn. We dare do nothing that might hurt the boy. The only thing that makes our lives worth living is the thought that one day, God knows how, he might return here to be crowned."

"*Our* lives?" Juniper echoed him. "How many of you are left?"

"There are seventy-eight of us—of those who served at your father's court—soldiers, servants, cooks, armorers like myself, wizards, and the rest. Some died trying to defend the castle against the knight's men. Some were . . ." he hesitated, ". . . made an example of. They were killed in dreadful ways to show the rest of us what we had to fear."

"I think we saw one such on the way here," Juniper said.

"Some have died of hunger or sickness in the winters since."

"Seventy-eight out of . . . maybe two hundred," Juniper said softly.

Lyon nodded. "We are a kind of outlaw," he said. "We have no proper work and no means of earning a living. We try to grow, catch, or fish a little food for ourselves and our children, but it is not usually enough. The farms that used to serve your father try to help us, but they have to give nearly everything they grow to Caerleon, and they do not have much themselves."

"Do you think about organizing yourselves into a rebellion?" Finbar asked.

"Against the Gray Knight's men?" Lyon smiled bitterly. "Our weapons and armor have been taken from us. We are just a rabble, and a disheartened rabble at that. The Gray Knight's army greatly outnumbers us." Lyon paused thoughtfully. "However, we see ourselves as a band of brothers and sisters. We share what food and skills we have. We are become a sort of family—even more so, perhaps, than in King Mark's time. Hardship and suffering have bonded us together."

"But anything you do would have to be done secretly," Juniper said, "so that the Gray Knight does not have wind of it. Does he have spies among you?"

Lyon looked at her with respect.

"There is only one spy as far as we know," he said. "Perquin, who acted as Brangwyn's regent. We believe he sent secret messages to Caerleon so that the knight took us when we were feasting. We had eaten richly and drunk deep, and when the warnings of the sentries came, it was too late for us to resist."

"And where is Perquin now?"

"He is effectively *regulus* here under the Gray Knight, though they pretend that he is under Prince Brangwyn. Castle Dore is too dull for him, however. He craves society, women, fine food, and drink. This broken little kingdom has not much to offer him. So he is away a lot, either at Caerleon or elsewhere. Only we never know when he will return."

"And he leaves underlings behind?"

"There is Beringer, who is officially in charge in his absence. And a troop of soldiers. Beringer is a homesick Welshman who does not seek trouble. The soldiers . . . it is hard to say. Sometimes they can be brutal, sometimes they share food with the children. They, too, are homesick."

Juniper listened to all this with her special quality of attention, then suddenly straightened her back.

"I would like to meet your band of brothers and sisters. Do they have a name?"

Lyon hesitated. I could tell that this was such sensitive information that even to this daughter of King Mark it was not easy to speak of the matter. Juniper was quick to understand this.

"Talk to them first. Tell them that I am here, with friends, and that if we can find a way to help, we will."

Lyon nodded.

"It seems to me that you have one advantage, perhaps only one, apart from your devotion to one another," Juniper said. "You know this countryside—every cave, forest, hollow tree, or place where a boat can be beached or hidden. It's not much, but it is something."

As Juniper spoke, I watched the faces of Lyon and Merrion coming alight. Juniper's sympathy, her understanding, her longing to help as well as her descent from

Mark and Erlain brought a sense of hope, even if none of the problems of the stricken community were solved.

Lyon gave a slight gesture of recognition, almost like a bow. He confided to me later that there was something in Juniper's clear thinking and confident speech that reminded him irresistibly of her father and of the happy times long gone.

"Meanwhile, forgive me, Lyon, is there somewhere we could sleep?" Juniper asked. "We came by ship, but we moored it a good distance away, and it is too far for us to return tonight. And we are all worn out."

"It would be an honor for us to have you here," Lyon said. "Although we have made our homes in the old workshops, we have kept the royal apartments intact, against Brangwyn's return. I think there would be room for all of you to sleep there if you wished."

We said our good-nights to Merrion and then followed Lyon across several courtyards to the more imposing buildings Juniper had indicated when we first arrived. Lyon opened a locked door. It was very dark inside, and until he put his torch on a sconce and lit some other candles, I could see very little. Soon the light revealed a high chamber with a table and chairs, then a whole suite of rooms that opened off a passage.

"We have taken some of the blankets," Lyon admitted shamefacedly. "We were very cold at first. Nothing else has been removed, I think."

"Quite right," said Juniper. "We shall manage."

After Lyon had left, we did manage. Some blankets remained. After dividing them among us, Juniper briskly pulled a tapestry down from the wall, which she herself used as a bed covering. She took up a sheep's fleece that had adorned the floor and gave it to Finbar.

"I am only surprised they did not take everything in the royal apartments," she said. "I would have."

Finbar smiled. "But you are a king's daughter," he said, teasing her. "We know about them. They are used to having their own way."

Juniper shook her head, and they both laughed.

"In any case, it was a matter of respect," he said. "And they needed to feel that the royal apartments were ready for Brangwyn's return."

Soon, exhausted and not a little hungry, we were all in bed—Wise Child and I in Juniper's childhood apartment, Cormac in a bed her nurse had once occupied, Finbar in the outer room on a pile of rugs on the floor covered by the fleece, and Juniper in her parents' bed. I was reflecting on how strange this homecoming was for her—at how much loss she had suffered since she had left Castle Dore all those years before—when I began to notice an idea flickering around in the back of my head. That and my empty stomach (I was no longer accustomed to hunger as I had once been) continued to keep me awake long after Wise Child had gone to sleep. Then, sudden as a stroke

of lightning, the idea reached me. The other images I had
seen in the scrying bowl!

I was desperate to tell Juniper, but I knew she was
tired and I did not want to wake her. Still, Juniper was not
like other people. She might rather be woken up. And in
any case, I could go and see.

I clambered out of bed and, feeling very cold, walked
along the passage. A very long passage it was, since Juniper
as a child had lived in what was almost a separate house
from her parents. It was eerie, too. Apart from the torch
Lyon had left in the sconce when we first entered, which,
in any case, had almost burned itself out, the passage was in
total darkness. I was relieved when I came at last to the
room where Juniper slept. It had a heavy carved door that
I could open only with difficulty. It creaked a little as I did
so. I stood just inside the door and waited.

"Who is that?" Juniper asked in a calm, wakeful tone,
and I could tell she had just been lying there in the dark,
wide awake.

"Colman."

"What is it? Are you ill?"

"No. I remembered something else. From the scrying. I thought it might be important. Too important to
wait for the morning."

"Indeed it might. Come and get into bed and tell me
about it."

Steering by Juniper's voice, I groped my way to the
bed and gratefully slid under the warm covers.

"It doesn't seem to make much sense," I said, "and I feel rather silly over the whole thing, but you might be able to make something of it."

"Yes."

"There were three things I remembered . . . I mean, apart from seeing the Wooden Palace all burned and Prince Brangwyn's face. There were the three things all in the same place, I think. There was a late afternoon sun, there was a very odd-shaped tree, a hazel tree, I think, and there was this strange hill—it looked too steep for a hill, but so it was—and it was there that the tree grew."

There was a silence after I said this, quite a long silence, and I was just thinking that what I had seen did not amount to a pocketful of withered beans and that Juniper would have to make some polite comment so as not to hurt my feelings, when she said, "You have no idea—how could you?—of the importance of what you have just told me."

Her voice broke a little with emotion, and I was transfixed there in the big bed, wondering what could possibly be coming next.

"The hazel tree and the tor were very important to *me*. They were part of my vocation as a *doran*. When I was a little girl, I kept dreaming about them, night after night, though in my dream there was a moon, not a sun. The dreams troubled me a lot, not because of the tree and the moon, but because of another sequence in the dream in which something terrible happened.

"Really because of that dream, I went to study with

Euny, the *doran* who trained me. And what did I discover? That Euny lived on a strange-shaped tor, farther north from here in the Outlands. Then—not immediately, because I was a dreamy girl who never noticed things, but after a few weeks—I realized that the hazel tree grew right outside Euny's hut. And when I did notice it, the moon was shining, exactly as in my dream."

"What happened about the terrible bit of the dream?" I asked.

"Eventually it happened, and it *was* terrible. Finbar was there, too. The Gray Knight had taken the shape of a great black dog and chased us. He would have caught us, too. But Finbar and I survived because of Euny and her magic. She taught me what to do and gave me the tools I needed to survive."

We were both silent after this extraordinary story. I'm a rather practical sort of person, I think. Despite my experience with the scrying, I'm not sure I really believe in magic. If anyone but Juniper had told me all this, I would have thought it a pack of nonsense.

"I can see how it was important *then*," I said. "But what can it mean *now*?"

"I wonder that myself," said Juniper. "What it makes me wonder is whether Euny can help us. Your vision suggests that she may be able to."

My vision! It seemed a very grand word for anything I was capable of having.

"I don't feel too comfortable about all this," I said. "I may have just made it up."

"It is strange, I know, but some people, and it seems as if you are one of them, sometimes do know things that it seems as if they cannot possibly know. You looked in the water, and you saw what you saw. It gives us a clue, no more than that. We must travel to the tor and see what it tells us."

I suddenly thought of Wise Child.

"I wish Wise Child had seen this instead of me."

"I know," Juniper said. "Poor girl, she has lost her way just at present."

"Will she find it again?"

"Almost certainly," said Juniper. "I have great faith in her. But this is a hard time for her."

I said, not sure whether I was being disloyal, "She says that being a *doran* is dangerous and that the idea frightens her."

"It is dangerous, some of the time. Be a good friend to her, Colman. She loves you and needs your friendship."

"I need hers," I said.

There was something else I needed to say to Juniper, something I could not have said to most people.

"You know, even now that it is burned and ruined, Castle Dore is very grand. I think I would have found it difficult to be here in the old days. It would have made me feel poor and unimportant."

Juniper made a sympathetic noise.

"I do know what you mean, of course," she said. "Try not to be taken in by things like great houses or money or splendor, Colman. Or grand people. Of course, all of us get taken in a bit, but it is all nonsense. Everyone—kings, rich people, clever people—is going to die one day just the same as poor people, and all the great buildings will fall into ruin. Kings and princes make their houses big so that others will feel small. Once you see that, they don't have so much power over you."

She suddenly added in an inconsequential way that was typical of her, "I bet you are hungry."

"I am!" I blurted out, and she laughed.

"I've just remembered there's an apple in my pocket over there. Aunt Brigid gave it to me. It's yours if you want it."

I took the apple (rather withered, as it was the lag end of winter), went back to bed with it, and munched on it gratefully. Finally I went to sleep.

CHAPTER THREE

I don't know whether Finbar slept much that night. Several times I heard him walking about, and at least once he quietly opened the outer door and went into the courtyard. Sailors are used to sleeping in short, intense snatches, which is often all that their work allows them, but I think it was more that he worried about the potential dangers of Castle Dore and felt responsible for our little party.

What I was beginning to learn about Finbar was that unlike most grown-up people, he lived entirely in the joys, fears, and excitements of whatever was going on. When he had been away at sea, he had given himself up to his ship and his men and to the excitements of trading in foreign places, regardless of having a little daughter at home who needed him. But now that he was home, or at any rate in Cornwall, we had his full attention for our adventure. We were his comrades and his family.

In spite of his wakeful night, he was the first up. He had a fire going in the old kitchen and was stirring oatmeal into a pan. Like all sailors, he could cook.

"Where did that food come from?" asked Juniper sleepily when she wandered in. "I'm so hungry."

"Lyon left a sack of oatmeal and some milk with me this morning," Finbar replied.

"They are generous," Juniper said. "I hope they are not going short because of it."

When we had eaten our porridge—a good-sized bowl of it each and (I must confess) the leavings for me—we had our council.

"Lyon is arranging a meeting for us with the outlaws to take place two days from now," Finbar began. "The outlaws are forbidden by the knight to meet in more than small numbers—about six, I think—so it has to be done secretly. They use a big cave with a lot of different exits and entrances, which the soldiers don't know about. Juniper, do you know—"

"The Cave of the Mermaids," she said.

"Yes, that's it," Finbar said. "They get together there to make their plans. It must be quite hard for them to trust us. It would be impossible if it were not for you, Juniper, and even now I think they are uncertain, not in their hearts, but in their minds, perhaps. They remember you with great affection, but you were a little girl then, and if you think of it from their point of view, they are not to know if you have changed in all the years or have even formed an alliance with the Gray Knight. I do not think this is what they believe, but they are right to be careful, since their lives depend upon it.

"The other side of the coin for them is that they need help, some new plan about what to do next. They are pretty desperate and also in a helpless position, and that is a terrible thing to be, since they are a proud people with an honorable history. Until the meeting they want us to stay hidden here. Under no circumstances can we let the soldiers know that new people have come and that one of them has old associations with Castle Dore."

"Good," said Juniper. "But I learned something last night that may make a difference."

Finbar looked at her in surprise. As far as he knew, she had seen no one since we'd left Lyon the evening before.

She went on. "Colman remembered something from the scrying, something important, though I don't yet know its full significance."

Juniper had a way of saying these things in a brisk, no-nonsense tone, which took away from the weirdness of what was being said and made it sound like something any sensible person would understand.

"It had features of my old childhood dream that drove me to train as a *doran* with Euny. Colman has not seen Euny's tor and her hazel tree any more than I had, and he knew nothing of my dream, yet he described the place to me.

"What I do not know is whether Euny is still alive. There was a rumor a few years ago, about the time of Brangwyn's capture, now that I think of it, that she had disappeared. In Euny's case, that would not necessarily mean she was dead. She was given to disappearing, often in broad daylight, which is something I always envied her. I've known only one other *doran* who could do it. Besides that, somehow I cannot imagine her dying without saying farewell to me. *Dorans* always know when they are going to die, often to within an hour or two, and they always inform their pupils. I am sure Euny would not have died without telling me."

"So what does this mean for us?" Finbar asked.

"I don't know exactly, but it probably means that we should try to find her."

"I see," said Finbar doubtfully.

"What I would like to do is set off at once. I would reach the tor before nightfall—it is in the Outlands to the north. If Euny is there, well and good. If not, perhaps there would be some clue for me from her."

"You cannot do that, Juniper," Finbar said very definitely. "You are the only one of us the outlaws recognize and trust as well as being a kind of symbol for King Mark and Prince Brangwyn. It would ruin things if you went away."

I suspect Finbar also thought, but did not say, that there were dangers for a woman wandering alone in that countryside with its soldiers and desperate subjects.

I could see Juniper weighing Finbar's words in her mind. She wanted to meet all the outlaws who had been beloved members of the Castle Dore family in her youth and to talk with them about what needed to be done. Yet to follow the trail of Euny, however insubstantial, offered her more real hope of being able to change their desperate situation.

I surprised myself by making a suggestion.

"If I somehow picked up your dream that connected you to Euny, do you think if I went I might pick up whatever else is to be found there?" I said. "I don't mind trying. And if I find nothing, you could always go yourself after the meeting."

Juniper looked at me and smiled. I did not dare look at Wise Child.

"You could be right," Juniper said. "But you cannot go alone. Cormac, would you go with him?"

"Of course," Cormac said.

"I will need to teach you the way, which is not difficult." Juniper began to draw a sketch with a knife on the sanded kitchen floor.

"You follow the river as far as the forest," she explained. "That will take you until mid-afternoon if you start soon. Then there is a track into the forest away to the left. Now and again you will get a glimpse of the tor away in the distance. It's a very odd shape, with almost vertical sides in places. You can't miss it. You keep bearing to the right until you come to a stream. You cross the stream, and there is a funny little wood and the tor beyond it. This is the shape of the tor, and here"—she drew an X—"is Euny's hut, unless it has fallen down by now. In front of it is, or was, the hazel tree."

The trouble was that we had almost nothing to take with us to eat. We had eaten a good breakfast but might not get the chance to eat again until another day, and the thought of the long walk there and back on two bowls of porridge was rather daunting. Finbar managed to find the heel of a loaf of bread he had forgotten in his pocket. We filled a leather flask with water and tried to put a brave face on it. Then we opened the door, and there on the step someone had left a large pasty.

"God bless them!" said Cormac. Juniper broke the pasty in half—it was full of meat and vegetables—and gave half to me and Cormac, which we tucked away in the pouch Cormac carried, along with the water.

"How will I know if I do come across clues?" I suddenly asked, my earlier confidence dissolving now that I was actually going to go.

Juniper gave me her best smile, one which somehow combined a knowledge of how funny and unexpected life was with a tender understanding that it was also quite difficult.

"Someone who can scry can probably recognize a clue when he sees one," she said reassuringly. "And if not, we will try again later. Just be open to whatever happens, attentive, not trying too hard. *You* know."

I knew it as soon as she said it. It was how I had been

when I saw the pictures in the scrying bowl, relaxed, not forcing anything.

She and Finbar and Wise Child watched us set off down the road. When we came to a turn in the track, I turned round and waved. The sight of Wise Child standing there—tense, unmoving, almost certainly unhappy—troubled me, and on an impulse I gave the curlew cry that had been our old signal in the days on the island. To my pleasure she acknowledged this with an uncertain wave.

Cormac was not the most talkative of companions, and I had always felt rather shy of him, though the closeness of our lives on the ship and at the farm had reduced this. He was someone, however, whom I instinctively trusted. Despite all that had happened to him, he was a generous spirit, a lover of life and of people. He was a good walker, too, and we swung along the river in fine style.

The day had the chilly promise of early spring. There was a brave blue sky and a constant movement of birds, some flying in and out of the trees with twigs and grasses in their beaks, intent on making their nests. At one point I burst into an old marching song we used to sing in the village, and Cormac joined in in a strong tenor. We looked at each other and smiled.

"It's funny to be looking for something when I don't know what it is," I remarked. "I have a nasty feeling Juniper is going to be disappointed in me."

"She's so often right, though," said Cormac. "I've been tempted sometimes to tell her she is talking nonsense, only I am too polite. But then she *isn't* talking nonsense. Hardly ever. I have just come to believe that she sees what I don't see, like a hawk sees what a sparrow can't."

It seemed odd to compare Juniper to something as fierce as a hawk, but yes, if life was about seeing from a different perspective, she certainly could do that.

Once in the forest, we sat down for a bit under a tree and ate some of our food. It was warmer now. The windflowers shone in the grass, and here and there a celandine showed its glossy yellow head.

"What do you think of our prospects against the Gray Knight?" I asked Cormac.

"On the face of it, we don't stand a chance," Cormac said. "He has the power. I gather he has been building his army for years. And according to Juniper, Meroot has *her* power, and of a pretty sinister kind. In Brangwyn they have a hostage that all of us—Juniper, the villagers—would do almost anything not to harm. They hold all the cards."

"So is there any hope?"

"Sometimes when people hold all the cards, they get too confident, too arrogant," Cormac said. "Like Goliath and the Philistines in the Bible. Then the unexpected happens, and they expose their weakness to their enemies. If we could spot the Gray Knight's weakness, perhaps we could knock him down with one pebble, as David did with the giant. People who do evil things often have blind spots that eventually destroy them."

"So we are going to look for the pebble?"

"Something like that."

We saw nobody in the forest—I don't suppose many people ever walked there. I was glad to have Cormac with me. Juniper had told us that when Euny had summoned her as a young girl to be her pupil, she had done this walk by herself, nervous of boars and brigands. At the last she had slipped on a stepping stone and fallen into a stream in the semi-darkness, arriving at Euny's hut dripping wet and with a sprained ankle. Juniper hadn't said much more about her subsequent life with Euny, but I gathered its discomforts had been quite a shock for a spoiled young princess.

Eventually we came to the stream and the stepping stones, the very place where poor Juniper had fallen, and we could see the tor stretching above us. The afternoon had an edge of darkness now, and the cold was returning. I looked forward to the hut, imagined going into it, and, if Euny was not there, lighting a fire to keep us warm. I even picked up some pieces of wood on the way.

We climbed the first stretch of the steep side of the tor, went through a clearing and past a huge oak tree, and there we were. Or rather we weren't. For beside a hazel tree, covered in its spring catkins, lay a pile of broken timbers.

I felt like bursting into tears. "There was no hut in my vision," I said. "Just a hazel tree and the sun." And indeed, just as in my dream, the late afternoon sun shone through the branches of the hazel tree.

"Whoever did this," Cormac said at length, "was in a violent mood."

It was true. The hut had been not merely pulled down but hacked in pieces by a huge ax. The raw splinters were everywhere.

"If Euny was here when they came," he went on, "she would not have stood a chance."

"Perhaps they were angry because she was *not* here," I said. "If, like Juniper, she could *see,* she might have known that they were coming and fled."

Standing helplessly by the ruins of the hut, Cormac and I picked up a few pieces of wood, but with no real hope of finding anything beneath them. It was the hut of a poor old woman who had owned very little, and now it had been destroyed.

I looked at the hazel tree and the warm sun shining through it and suddenly felt a sense of hope. My eyes traveled up the steep side of the tor.

"I think we should climb the hill," I said.

Cormac looked surprised. "Why?" he asked.

"I'm not sure," I said honestly.

Cormac took me at my word, and we started up the mountain, an almost vertical climb. Soon we were both panting and had to stop many times to get our breath. Then, some ways above us in the darkening air, we could see the outline of a small wattle building.

We applied ourselves to the last difficult scramble, searching for toe and hand holds on stony outcroppings in the rough grass. It felt precarious, as if any minute we might start rolling down the hill and not stop until we fell into the stream at the bottom. With a last heave, we pulled ourselves up to a flat piece of ground in front of the hut and lay there gasping, gazing outward and downward over a wide view.

Finally we got our breath and stood before the little door of the hut. It yielded easily as we lifted the latch, and we moved in. At once we became aware of the atmosphere. It was a shrine—that was obvious—and in the center of the shrine was the most unforgettable figure.

She sat on a throne in a cave that had been built for her. She was, in a way, hideous—crudely carved and painted, with wild black eyes set in a grimy face. She wore a crown made of moon and stars and a gown of vivid blues and reds. She carried a baby at her breast. Someone had placed a garland of greenery around her neck—windflowers, already drooping, wound into a necklace of ivy. She was surrounded by small pots of flowers—some of them quite fresh, I noticed—and other little offerings—a cheese, some milk, some bread. Nearby, in the floor of the hut, stood a well, and around its rim many candles had been set.

Before the little figure—so small, so ugly, so ancient, so dignified—was a worn place in the earthen floor. There was another worn place on her outstretched foot. It occurred to me that people must prostrate themselves there in order to kiss the foot, and that their kisses had worn away the wood from which she was carved.

Cormac and I glanced at each other, fascinated and uncomfortable, wondering what the other thought.

A sudden impulse, embarrassing but unstoppable, seized me, and in front of Cormac I knelt down on the earth floor, leaned forward, and kissed the foot. For I knew that I was in the presence of a deity, and that such a deity commanded love and obedience. Cormac then did the same.

"What now?" I asked Cormac after a long silence.

"We could spend the night here," he said.

"Do you think she would mind?"

"We could ask her to forgive us for sleeping in her presence. Since we have nowhere else to go. It will be horribly cold tonight out on that hillside."

"We should make her an offering."

Cormac produced what was left of our pasty. "Suppose we gave her half of this and ate the other half?" he said. This would leave us rather short of provisions on the way home, but I knew that what was given to gods and goddesses had to cost you something. This was what showed your devotion.

We placed the pasty in front of her on the floor (Oh, the rich smell of it to our hungry nostrils! I thought, "We must be mad to give this away!") and poured out a little of our water.

"Mother," I said, as if I had been talking this sort of language all my life. "We offer you our devotion, we thank you for your hospitality, since we have nowhere else to go this night, and we beg you to accept our tiny offering of food and drink as our recognition of your majesty."

Where did these words come from? They certainly amazed me.

Now Cormac spoke. "We come as friends of the *doran* Juniper, who was trained by the *doran* Euny," he said. "We are seeking a way to right a great wrong, and we crave your indulgence for sharing your palace."

Exhausted by so much piety and starving hungry, Cormac and I then set to and demolished the rest of the pasty, leaving us with only the dry heel of bread to sustain us on the journey home. There was a tinderbox in the corner, and Cormac lit some of the candles, which flickered over the face of the little goddess until sometimes I thought I could see her expression change or fancied she was about to speak. It was quite warm in the hut, and the pasty had quieted my hunger. I felt as if I might want to lie and watch the little goddess forever. It seemed a shame that my eyelids were so heavy.

"I'll just sleep for a minute or two," I thought, "and then enjoy watching the goddess some more."

It was dawn when I woke. The rays of the sun lit the face of the goddess with an expression of great tenderness and illuminated the little building with a gold radiance, though the light had a misty quality about it, as if the goddess was partly concealed from us. Cormac was asleep beside me. I lay there contentedly, surprised how the time had passed, when suddenly a shock ran through me. I had had a dream!

Little fragments of it came to me first, and then a fuller memory of it overwhelmed me. I had dreamed that I was lying on the floor there, and that the goddess had got up from her throne and come to me, touching my face and calling me by my name. I had gazed up at her in admiration.

"You and your friends are in great trouble," she had said. "There will be danger, there will be deeds of high heroism, and you will be afraid. I want you to take the protections that I will give you. Rightly used, they will keep you all safe."

Then I noticed that she was carrying an object in her hand—a black egg. She put it down beside me. "Guard it well!" she said.

She produced a liquid in a glass flask—not the clearwater that Juniper and Wise Child used in situations of danger, but a deep red-purple liquid, the color of wine. "This is for your enemies—not for you!" she said.

She handed me a tiny glass bottle, which appeared to have a scrap of fabric inside it. "This needs great care. Juniper will explain it." She also picked up what looked like a bundle of sticks with leaves and gave them to me.

Finally, she reached into her gown and produced a

tiny silver crescent moon on a leather thong—Juniper had one just like it—and put it around my neck.

"It is the task of the *doran* to mend that which is broken and to find that which is lost," she said in her beautiful, deep voice. "You are not yet a *doran,* and you have a path to tread before you know whether you will be."

I was overwhelmed by the beauty of this dream as I remembered it. My hand went to my neck to find the crescent moon, and I was bitterly disappointed to find that there was nothing there. I looked wildly around the floor for the egg, the bundle of sticks, the flask of liquid, and the tiny bottle. There was no sign of them. My cry of despair woke Cormac, and I told him all that had happened to me.

"I had a dream, too," he told me. "It was that my face was restored, that I looked as I did before. I guess that has not happened either."

I shook my head.

"It is odd," Cormac said, "because I feel that I trust her."

"Let's go," I said, not having the heart to discuss it further. We tied on our shoes, picked up our pouch, and stood up. On an impulse I knelt again before the goddess and kissed her once more. Cormac did the same. We turned and left. And there, on the doorstep of the little building, arranged neatly together, was a black egg, a flask of purple liquid, a tiny bottle, a bundle of twigs with leaves on them, and a silver crescent on a thong.

We gazed at each other, not speaking. I picked up the crescent moon and put it on. We put the other things carefully away in our pouch and set off down the mountain.

By evening we were back at Castle Dore. I wondered how I would describe the strange thing that had happened to me. It felt so solemn—this is an odd thing to say, I know—that I was afraid I would burst out laughing as I told it.

In fact, the opposite happened. Sitting in the kitchen of the old royal apartments, with all their eyes upon me, I suddenly began to cry. I felt babyish and ashamed.

"We have not had much to eat today," Cormac said protectively. "We are both tired out by all that happened."

"Something did happen, then?" Juniper asked.

"Indeed it did."

I could see Juniper's eyes on the crescent moon, which had dropped out of my shirt; she had known the answer to her question before she asked it.

"So is Euny alive?" I could feel the longing in her voice. I looked at Cormac, wanting him to tell the story while I recovered myself. He described the broken hut and the savagery with which it had been attacked. Interestingly, after a shudder, Juniper responded to that exactly as I had done.

"Perhaps they were angry because she was not there?"

Cormac described the stiff climb up to the tiny shrine

on the top of the tor, and I could see Juniper reliving similar visits she had made with Euny.

"It was very beautiful," he said simply. "We felt full of reverence for . . . whoever the goddess is. I think we both felt we loved her. We made her an offering—half our pasty and some water. We asked her indulgence to let us sleep at her shrine because it was too cold to sleep out on the hillside."

There was a pause. To me Cormac said, "You tell the rest."

Haltingly, overcome with emotion and troubled by Wise Child's fierce little face glaring at me ("This should have happened to her," I thought), I told my story. I described the blissful dream, the gifts, and then the sharp disappointment of finding that the gifts had gone.

"So we made our reverences to her and left," I said. "Then"—my voice broke, and I started to cry again—"the gifts were piled upon the doorstep."

"Could we see them?" Juniper asked gently. Cormac lifted them from the pouch and laid them one by one upon the table. They looked oddly insignificant lying there—a flask of wine, a black egg, some twigs, and a little bottle.

"She said you would know about using them," I said.

"The drink will paralyze someone," Juniper said immediately. "Not forever, of course, but for a good many hours. The black egg is very powerful. Finbar, do you remember?"

"You used one just like it against the Gray Knight. It saved us," Finbar said gruffly.

Juniper nodded. "It is to be thrown at an enemy at the moment of ultimate danger—neither before nor after. The bottle is what is called the cloth of disguise. The idea is that it gives you time to escape. The twigs I shall have to think about. I cannot quite remember their use, but it will come back to me. Best protection of all, in my view, is the silver moon."

She brought out her own from beneath her gown. "This was given to me by Euny when I completed my training as a *doran*. It has its own ways of warning, as well as being a protection. Colman, you will go more safely into danger because of it."

"I'd like to understand this better," said Finbar, sounding a shade irritated. "We are faced with armies, swords—the might of the Gray Knight—against a broken rabble of hungry and desperate outlaws. As powerful as they are, will it not take more than black eggs and flasks of magic liquid to save the situation?"

"We are also faced with the magic—the bad magic—of Meroot and the Gray Knight," said Juniper firmly. "That is also a threat, one we must not underestimate. You know that as well as I do, Finbar. Tomorrow when we meet the outlaws, we shall need to talk of these things. Now, I think, Colman and Cormac should go to their beds. They must be worn out."

I drank some soup Juniper had made and went thankfully to bed. I noticed that Wise Child had not even said good night to me.

CHAPTER FOUR

I was awakened early the next morning by the sound of Finbar moving around the kitchen, and I stumbled out of bed to join him. This was a special day, the day of our meeting with the outlaws.

"Just thought I'd make us a little something before the meeting," he said, stirring the porridge cauldron. "Juniper is getting herself ready."

I don't think either of us was prepared for Juniper's appearance when she came in. For weeks now, apart from the few shawls and wraps Aunt Brigid had lent her, we had only seen her in the old black dress she had worn at the trial. Now suddenly she was transformed. She wore a tunic in peacock silk with greeny blue colors that shifted in the light. Beneath it she wore a black skirt. At her waist was an embroidered belt set with jewels of lapis and turquoise that matched the changing colors of the silk. Around her neck she wore a high collar, jeweled with garnets, and her black hair—smooth, oiled perhaps—was wound upward onto her head and held in a glittering comb. She wore huge rings on her fingers and fine kid boots on her feet.

Finbar and I stared in amazement.

"I looked through Erlain's things," Juniper explained, slightly embarrassed. "I am taller than her, but I think it looks all right, don't you?"

"You don't think . . ." Finbar was hesitant. "You don't think that it is a little fine for a bunch of outlaws who have barely enough to eat?"

Juniper considered. "In order to trust us," she said, "they have to feel that I am part of the old world of King Mark. If I look like Erlain, if I remind them of those good times, don't you think it will help? Seeing me in my old rags cannot do much to convince them of my heritage."

"You may be right," said Finbar. "I just don't know."

For my part, I thought Juniper looked wonderfully regal. In the long weeks of the trial, the escape, and her illness, I had forgotten her great dignity and grace.

While we ate, Juniper briefly told us that even if we children got bored, it was important that we made a good impression and sat as quietly as we could. This was so unlike Juniper—she rarely told us to behave ourselves—that we took it very seriously.

"This is about the future of these people and their children," she said, "and for that matter, the future of my brother, Brangwyn. So, of course, it matters a lot."

Perhaps because we were impressed at how much trouble Juniper had taken with her clothes, we all made some effort with our appearance. Finbar trimmed his beard, he and Cormac and I put on clean shirts, and Wise Child took up a crimson scarf Juniper had discarded in her search and wound it about her neck. The color suited her.

I was curious about how the cave could remain so well hidden from the soldiers, but I soon discovered the answer. To begin with, the five of us walked along the cliff top. After about five minutes we came to three enormous rocks set at angles to one another. Juniper climbed nimbly up one of these and disappeared into the heart of the rock formation. Less nimbly, we followed her and found ourselves in a grassy space between them all. A much smaller rock was wedged between two of the bigger ones. Juniper climbed over this and the rest of us followed. Behind us, under the rock we had just climbed, was a small, dark tunnel, little more than a hole, really. Juniper took down a lamp and a tinderbox from a shelf inside the cave and carefully lit the lamp. As we each wriggled through the hole, we could see that a dry path wound downward at our feet.

"Keep close together," Juniper said, "and mind you don't trip." It was good advice because it was a rocky path that continued steadily downward, quite sharply in places, so that we felt as if were falling rather than walking. What impressed me was that there were a number of turnings off the path on both sides that Juniper ignored. Then she did take one of the turnings, and then another turning off that turning, until I was quite bewildered. Eventually we emerged into a much taller and wider passage. Far ahead of us we could see the faint lights of the Cave of the Mermaids and hear the echoing murmur of talk.

The moment we entered the Cave of the Mermaids, there was a gasp of surprise and pleasure from the waiting outlaws at Juniper's appearance. I felt quite shy emerging into the huge cave with the eyes of so many people upon us, but Juniper carried herself, as she always did, superbly. While the outlaws stared, she showed us where to sit, and then, without being invited, moved to a seat that stood high up as if it were a throne. With one accord the outlaws stood until she had taken her seat.

Blinking, I looked around. The cave was marvelous, like a great hall carved out of stone. A dazzling crack of light came in through the wall behind Juniper and illuminated the wall opposite, the stones of which were a brilliant green with white veins running through them. Through the crack I could faintly hear the sound of the sea. Rock formations descending in layers from the walls provided seating. Whether the people had worked on the stone to make these more comfortable, I do not know. High in the walls they had placed sconces that held candles, which made the chamber brilliant with light and unexpectedly warm.

The outlaws themselves were not an impressive sight. There were perhaps sixty of them in the cave. Finbar later told me that some had remained at home, either to mind children or so that if the Gray Knight's soldiers came, life would seem to be going on as normal in the farms and workshops of Castle Dore. They bore all the marks of poverty, hunger, and the unremitting toil required simply to survive under the tyranny of the Gray Knight. I contrasted this with the world of Castle Dore that Juniper had described to us—a peaceful, happy place where the farms yielded the people a comfortable living. Yet there was an attitude about the outlaws—of dignity and determination— that did perhaps show the spirit of people who had once known freedom and a good life.

"I am very grateful to you," Juniper began in her beautiful, deep voice, "for granting me and my friends the courtesy of this meeting—at great risk to yourselves, as I know very well. I am appalled at the sufferings and hardships that you and your families have already endured, and it is plain that whatever we decide to do now will need the utmost caution and discretion. I want you to know that my friends Finbar, Cormac, Colman, and Wise Child," she said, indicating us each in turn, "would like to do everything in their power to help and support you and my brother, Prince Brangwyn, and to break the power of the Gray Knight. It cannot be easy for you to trust us, but as you remember me in the old days, as you remember my parents, I beg you to believe that our whole wish is to help. We are your friends and will do anything we can to make things better and to free your future king."

The oldest of the men then stood. His name was

Cremon, and his gnarled face illustrated the pain and hardship of the last few years. "It is for me to welcome you and your friends, Princess," he said. "We remember your father and mother with great love and admiration and think with longing of the old days. We remember you, too, as a young princess. I think I speak for everyone here when I say that we do not believe that you come to harm us, but that our situation is so dangerous that it would be possible for you to destroy us without even meaning to. As you know, we exist in a wretched state of bondage to Caerleon, and we find ourselves powerless. We have no weapons and very little food. We are constantly visited by the Gray Knight's soldiers and the traitorous Perquin, and we live in fear of bringing harm to Prince Brangwyn. None of us knows how it really fares with him, or whether at any time our meager supplies of food may be cut off and our families starved. In such a situation it is difficult to find hope, although we do not lack courage or determination."

Juniper nodded then, in that very definite way she has, as if she has taken in all possibilities but yet has more to say.

"I would hate you to think," she said, "that as newcomers we wanted to push our way blindly into this very painful situation, which you understand in a way we cannot. We would do nothing without consulting you first. Would you feel it impertinent, however, if, as a newcomer but also as King Mark's daughter, I made suggestions—

suggestions you could take up or ignore, as you wished?"

"Of course," old Cremon said. "We would be glad to listen to anything you have to say."

"There is the question of arms," she said. "You must, of course, have arms to defend yourselves and your families. My companion Finbar has a ship harbored not very far away, though well hidden. It would be possible for him to sail to another country—Ireland, perhaps, where they are famous for their swords and armor—and buy enough weapons to arm each of you. He would then sail into your own harbor here one night and distribute them, if we were sure the soldiers were away."

As Juniper spoke, I began to notice the outlaws sitting up straighter. No doubt they were listening to the first good news they had had for months.

"That takes money," old Cremon said, "and we have no money."

"Leave that to me," said Juniper. "I think I can find what is needed."

A ripple of anticipation ran around the cave. Here was a more powerful ally than they had dreamed of.

"I am not, of course, suggesting that you challenge the army of Caerleon in battle," Juniper went on. "Only that if conditions were right and necessary, you should be appropriately armed. I believe that other work needs to be done first. For example, it might be possible for one or two of us to infiltrate Caerleon Castle and find out more about our enemies. Not Finbar or myself, I think. Meroot would almost certainly recognize us, though it is many years since we last met. But we need to know more about how Prince Brangwyn is kept, whether he is drugged or threatened, whether he dreams of escape. We need much more information about the hopes and fears of the Gray Knight and Meroot. 'Know your enemy' is always a good rule."

One of the women spoke. "One or two of our people, including some children, have already been taken to the castle, Princess, and forced to work there as chambermaids and kitchen workers. We have always tried to avoid such close contact with the castle. It did not occur to us that it might be useful, and in any case, the workers are rarely allowed out and never allowed to return home, so we receive no information."

"Still, it might be useful to know someone inside the castle," Juniper said. "Also, you may know that I am a *doran*, one who believes in a special sort of power. At first sight it has little to do with soldiers and armies, still less with the sort of power that Caerleon represents, though, of course, the Gray Knight and Meroot also use a kind of magic, different from mine. In the end I believe that my sort of power is stronger than theirs, though it needs the most careful sort of application and may not achieve results quickly."

It was astonishing the way Juniper's energy and confidence ran through the poorly dressed, beaten-looking bunch of outlaws. They sat up, smiled at one another, and began to ask questions and to make suggestions.

"The soldiers never come here at night if there isn't a moon," someone said. "We think they are afraid of being attacked in the dark."

"We'd all feel much better with a sword in our hands," said another.

"Magic? That's women's business, isn't it?"

"Not necessarily."

"Does it work?"

"Wait and see!"

"Getting into Caerleon? I don't know that I'd care to do that."

"I have stayed at Caerleon myself," Juniper volunteered. "Finbar, too. As a girl, I went on an official visit to Caerleon, with Finbar as my attendant. Our real reason was to smuggle out a friend of ours whom Meroot was ill-treating. We spirited him away by way of the stream that runs through the heart of the castle."

"What was Caerleon like?" one of the outlaws asked.

"Deadly quiet. I remember the eerie silence of the place, quite unlike Castle Dore. Meroot and the Gray Knight control those who work for them by terrorizing them. There was a lot of spying—looking through holes in doors and walls and tapestries. I would have been more scared if I had been old enough to know how much danger I was in."

For a long time I listened to the people talking, to Juniper talking, to Finbar talking, and then I began to get a bit bored. I remembered what Juniper had said about behaving ourselves, otherwise I might have started ragging around with Wise Child, but then a terrible sleepiness began to overwhelm me, and I suspect Wise Child, too. I think I must have started to snore because I woke up suddenly to find everyone looking at me and laughing, and I went horribly red.

"I think I must take these two home," said Juniper. "I will set them on their way and return."

Still drowsy, we stumbled after her and began the steep upward climb out of the cave with all its muddling side paths.

"Where do they go to?" Wise Child asked Juniper.

"To other caves and to a warren of passages," said Juniper. "We were never allowed to come down here alone as children—it is so easy to get lost and there are dozens of passages, some of which end in dangerous precipices and crumbling rock faces."

Together we made the last scramble up to the surface and squeezed through the hole at the top.

"You know your way from here," Juniper said.

"Of course," said Wise Child impatiently.

I was surprised at how much of the day had gone by. The sun was fairly low in the sky. The bright morning in which we had set off full of curiosity and nervousness had faded into a dull afternoon, and a kind of gloom fell on both of us. We walked back to the royal apartments without talking. We ate some bread and cheese and drank a little milk. Suddenly we heard the sound of horses' hooves on the cobbles outside. Wise Child and I looked at each other first with astonishment, then with fear. I peeped out, unseen, I hoped, and saw perhaps ten soldiers on horseback.

They circled the buildings that surrounded the royal apartments a number of times. At one moment when the sound of hooves retreated a little, Wise Child and I went with one accord and quietly shot home the bolts on the apartments' doors.

"They won't expect to find anyone here," I whispered to her. There was no need to whisper, but I could not help myself. "No one *has* lived here, after all, since Prince Brangwyn was taken away. Lucky we lit no candles."

Wise Child nodded, tense with listening. Just then someone tried the handle on the locked door! A little later we heard the soldiers shouting at someone—Lyon's wife, perhaps. After that, it was silent.

We sat still for a long time, afraid to move.

"What happens," Wise Child finally asked, "if the soldiers are around when the outlaws start coming out of the Cave of the Mermaids? They are not supposed to meet in groups of more than six. They could catch them and punish them."

We knew that the outlaws' deliberations were due to

end in the early evening so that they could make their way home in cover of darkness.

"I expect they have the sense to come out just a few at a time," I said.

"Yes, but sixty men and women wandering the lanes within an hour or so? Won't that seem very suspicious?"

I could see that it would. "But there's nothing we can do," I said miserably.

"We could warn them," Wise Child said with unexpected firmness.

"How?"

"Go back to the cave and tell them what has happened."

"Are you crazy?" I said. "Even if we could get to the entrance of the cave without meeting any of the soldiers, we would never find our way through that rabbit warren of paths. You heard what Juniper said."

"I could find the way," Wise Child said.

"That's nonsense. You'd lose yourself and no one would be helped at all. You'd just have made things worse."

"I *know* I could find the way."

It was true that Wise Child was rather good at finding the way to places, but this seemed to me entirely different.

"Impossible," I said. "They must take their chances."

Just as if I had not spoken, Wise Child went on, "We could go out by the back entrance here. There's a bit of garden, then a wood, then you can get up onto the cliff. The top of the cliff is full of rabbit holes. I cannot see soldiers taking horses up there in the dark."

"But the *path* to the cave," I said. "You will never find the path."

"Yes, I will," said Wise Child, not, it must be said, stubbornly or willfully, but as if in total confidence.

"Think!" I said in agony. "Think of the dangers!"

"I really don't think there will be any dangers once I am away from the soldiers, and with any luck, they are elsewhere by now."

"You are crazy," I said again, collapsing on a settle in my agitation.

"Colman! Listen to me! I *know* that I can do this."

She looked me full in the face in a way that reminded me of the old Wise Child, which affected me very much. There was a long silence between us, and then I said, "Well, I suggest we put a few things in a pouch—a bit of bread and some water, an apple or two—just in case you are not as wonderful as you think you are."

Wise Child laughed. "Good idea!" she said.

"Suppose we'd better get going," I said.

"We?"

"You don't think I'd let you go alone?"

"Colman! Even though you think I am bound to get you lost?"

"Well, you are so silly," I mumbled.

78

"Wait and see how silly I am." Wise Child seemed to have a new energy as she moved about the room getting herself ready to go. "But it will be lovely to have you with me."

I insisted that we leave a message for Juniper and Finbar. On a tablet that our Irish friends had given us, I carefully scrawled the information about where we had gone. Wise Child waited patiently while I did this, humoring me, I felt. Then I slipped my hand into my shirt and took off the silver crescent moon on the leather thong that hung round my neck. "I want you to wear this," I said.

Wise Child only hesitated for a moment, and then she took it from me, slipped it over her head, and tucked it into her clothes.

It was almost completely dark when we crept out into the overgrown and neglected garden. Both of us, we admitted later, felt that someone would be waiting to pounce on us out there, but, of course, no one did. At first we felt blinded by the dark, but then gradually our eyes grew accustomed to it. We found our way to the path through the wood, our ears all the time finely attuned to the jingle of harness or the sound of hooves, but there was nothing. Soon, after a scramble, we were up on top of the cliff, the sea a vast, luminous presence beneath us, the sky in patches of light and darkness, the air wonderfully fresh. I dreaded exchanging this dark, beautiful landscape for the treacherous and deceptive underground paths.

Quite quickly we found the three great rocks that hid

the entrance. We slid through the hole, and then, not without difficulty, managed to use the tinderbox to light the lamp. I tried not to keep saying, "Are you sure this is the right way?" because within a very few moments I realized that I had not the faintest idea which path was the one to take. Wise Child had, of course, taken the lead. I wished that I was walking in front of her so that I could have turned round and, quite casually, looked at the silver moon on the leather thong to see what it looked like. Juniper had told us that whereas at ordinary times it burned with a pale lavender light that was barely perceptible, in times of danger it shone with a vivid red light.

Wise Child seemed to have no problem, however. At each juncture she unerringly chose the next path and continued to walk forward quite briskly. I saw no sign of hesitation. Was this just bravado, I could not help wondering? How *could* she know what she was doing? After we had walked for a while, I became convinced that it was taking us much longer than it had with Juniper, and I resigned myself to the inevitable discovery that we were lost. I congratulated myself on the half a loaf and the flask of water we had tucked into the pouch I carried. That would keep us going for a bit, and maybe local people who had known these caves all their lives would eventually discover the two of us, still alive, I hoped.

I continued to revolve these gloomy thoughts while I marched loyally behind Wise Child until (surely my ears deceived me?) it seemed to me that I heard voices in the distance. The passage widened and grew taller, we circled some rocks, and then, all of a sudden, there we were in the Cave of the Mermaids! I have never forgotten the sight of all those people gazing at us in astonishment, as if we had come out of the ground itself.

"Wise Child!" said Juniper, her eyes fixed in surprise upon her pupil's face.

"I am sorry to interrupt you all," Wise Child said in a loud, confident voice that carried to every corner of the cave, "but we thought we should inform you that the soldiers have arrived at Castle Dore. They did not see us, because we were hiding in the royal apartments, but they galloped around and tried the door. We do not know where they are now. We thought that you should know this because if you all left the cave together, they might be suspicious."

There was a silence after this speech, and then old Cremon said, "You are brave, clever children, both to think of the risk we might be running and also to make your way down here to find us. Thanks to you, we shall leave the cave in very small numbers—some of us will now need to stay here all night. I cannot tell you how grateful we are for your concern on our behalf."

"Wise Child," said Juniper. "How did you find your way here?"

"I remembered it," said Wise Child, without sounding

as if she were boasting. "I just knew where to go."

Juniper said nothing more, but I had a feeling the subject was not exhausted between them.

The meeting at once began to break up. A small group of the outlaws prepared to leave by another entrance to the cave in the opposite direction from Castle Dore. Juniper, Wise Child, myself, and Lyon set off back the way we had come. Finbar and Cormac decided to stay behind to talk some more about the question of arms. This time Juniper led us, silently.

At the entrance to the cave we made our way along the cliff top the way we had come. As we turned into the garden of the royal apartments, I suddenly thought I could hear on the wind, far away up on the hill, the jingle of bits and the sound of hooves.

"We will not light any candles tonight," said Juniper, who had not commented on this noise. "We will talk for a little and then go to bed." Not unnaturally, she seemed tired from her long day.

Wise Child, on the other hand, walked with the confident swing of the hips that I remembered from of old. It had always meant that she was in a happy mood.

After we had sat down in the royal apartments, Juniper said, "That was an extraordinary feat, Wise Child! In my childhood we said that it took a child of Castle Dore a whole year to learn the path to the cave, and some took longer than that."

"How long did you take?" Wise Child asked curiously.

"Less than a year, but more than seven months. So you can understand my surprise."

I could feel Wise Child struggling with thoughts and words. "I don't know that I can explain it to you," she finally said. "When you led us down into the cave that first time, it was as if I could see a map of the whole cave in my mind, and on that map I marked the path that we had taken. I did not even think about it very much. I was not trying to learn it, because I did not expect to need to know it, or not so soon. Then, when Colman and I heard the soldiers and I saw the danger the outlaws were in, it seemed perfectly obvious what I must do. Colman offered to come with me, which was brave of him because he was sure I did not really know the way. He insisted that we take food and water."

Juniper listened carefully to this. I don't know what she was thinking, but what struck me was that it was the first time since we left the island that Wise Child had sounded truly like her old self, not cross or difficult or whining. She did not speak with a trace of pride in her extraordinary achievement. She was trying to tell us, as plainly as she could, exactly what had happened, and why, for her, it had seemed quite ordinary.

"Do you realize what this means?" Juniper said at last.

"What?" asked Wise Child.

"What you are describing is a gift of the *dorans*—and

only of one or two of them. As you know, we have many
different gifts between us. Ever since we left the island, it
seems to me that you have tried to forget that you used to
want to be a *doran*. You would not even attempt the scrying, though it was important to me then to have your help.
You have been sulky and miserable. On another occasion
I might have sent you to visit the shrine of the Mother,
but in the state of mind you were in, it would have been
useless. You would have found nothing. Yet now, suddenly,
something has changed."

Juniper spoke, as always, without a note of rebuke.
She was trying to describe exactly what had happened. I
waited for an outburst from Wise Child, but none came. In
just the same tone of voice in which she had described how
she had found the cave, she answered Juniper.

"I was afraid, that was why," Wise Child said. "I had
been rather excited, and proud, at the idea of being a
doran. It seemed to make me special, and I wanted to be
special. But then . . ." Wise Child's voice faltered. "Then I
saw what they did to you on the island, and I knew what
worse things they intended to do, and I got scared. If I
became a *doran*, I thought, that could happen to me. So I
made up my mind not to be one.

"There were other things, too, of course. Finbar was
not quite the father I had remembered, though I am getting used to him again now. And I was jealous of Colman.
I felt maybe you loved him more than you loved me.

Sorry!" She looked at me apologetically. "I couldn't seem to help it."

I had never felt so much love and admiration for her. However maddening she could be, Wise Child had always had a marvelous way of being suddenly and beautifully herself, and this was one such moment. I would have forgiven her anything. Juniper must have felt something similar, but she simply said, with a bit of a laugh in her voice, "Right, then. You are back to being my apprentice *doran* again, and I can tell you that I shall expect rather more obedience than I've seen from you lately!"

In order to show that this was, and wasn't, a joke, Juniper held out her arms to Wise Child, and Wise Child warmly hugged her in return, and even though it was dark by now, and we had no candles, I could sense that in the darkness both of them were smiling and smiling.

CHAPTER FIVE

"**W**hat if the soldiers catch us?" Cormac asked. We were sitting round, the five of us, having a late breakfast and talking of our impressions of the day before. "Sooner or later we are bound to run into them, and they will probably recognize that we are not Castle Dore people."

"Perhaps not in the case of the children," said Juniper, nodding at Wise Child and me. "The soldiers probably see the local children as a kind of mob. There are a lot of them."

"But they would recognize ours as outsiders if they heard them speak," put in Finbar.

"I can't see what alternative we have but to try to stay out of their way and hope for the best," Juniper said.

There was silence between us as we all considered a number of unpleasant possibilities. Me, I could not forget the nasty moment when they were trying the handle of the royal apartments while Wise Child and I lay trembling inside.

Cormac suddenly said, "The soldiers have gone from

the village, by the way. I crept out early this morning and had a word with Lyon, and he said that they left in the night. What he also said, however, was that Perquin is expected to visit in a week. When he does so, the whole community will be called together on the grass outside Castle Dore and given a speech of threats and warnings designed to make them feel more intimidated."

"I'd like to hear that," said Juniper. "Find out what sort of thing he says."

"Too risky," Finbar said. "You are too tall to blend in as a native, even though you are one."

"*We* could go, however," said Wise Child. "We could get Lyon to take us along as if we were his grandchildren. Juniper said herself that probably all the children look alike to the soldiers."

"I don't like the idea," Finbar said, his eyes on Wise Child.

"They'd blend in all right," said Cormac. "You'd need to get hold of those rusty-colored jerkins the children here wear. I 'specially noticed that they all seem to have them."

Juniper listened to all this and nodded slowly. One of the things I have always admired about her is that unlike most grown-ups, she is not in the habit of feeling that children must never do anything dangerous, though occasionally she says a warning word or two. My dad would have rejected out of hand something as risky as our going to hear

Perquin, partly to show that he was in charge and we had to do what he said.

"I want to talk about the business of arms," said Finbar. "When we discussed the possibility of my going to buy weapons and armor for the outlaws yesterday, you said that cost would not be a problem. What did you mean? Good quality weapons are expensive things, as you must well know."

"Oh yes!" said Juniper, as if he had just reminded her of something she had forgotten. "Come with me!"

Intrigued, we followed her into what had been her parents' bedroom and then out of it again into the huge closet, almost a room, where Erlain had kept her clothes. There was a press, a huge piece of furniture made of some rare pale wood that contained a brilliant array of Erlain's dresses. Juniper pushed these aside to reveal a large panel of beautifully grained wood. For a moment, as she ran her fingers along the grain and pushed against the panel, Juniper seemed perplexed. Then suddenly the panel began to slide under her fingers, revealing a dark hole in which we could dimly see large leather bags. Juniper heaved out one of the bags—it was obviously very heavy—untied the lacing round the top, and took out a handful of gold coins.

"There is plenty more," she said simply. "This was my father's safe place. No one knows of it but me and possibly Brangwyn. And now all of you."

I became aware that my mouth was hanging open and hastily closed it again.

"Well!" said Finbar. "That will certainly pay for weapons for the men of Castle Dore. In fact, it would pay to hire a troop of soldiers to fight on Castle Dore's behalf!"

"I know," said Juniper.

"But you did not mention it yesterday."

"I am not sure yet that that is the way forward."

Finbar nodded.

"We need to know more about Brangwyn and other things. And we need the people here to feel that they are in charge of their destiny. The worst thing that has happened to them is to be made to feel powerless. So let us see about weapons first, and then we could discuss whether we need to pay men to fight for us. I have to say that if men are going to fight, I would rather they did it out of conviction than for money."

"Even if they lost the battle because there were not enough soldiers?" Finbar said.

"No, I would not want them to lose," said Juniper. "But let's leave that for a bit. The immediate question is, how do we get all that heavy money onto your ship?"

"There are a number of donkeys in the village," Cormac said. "Probably four bags would cover your expenses—six, to be on the safe side. If we could distribute the weight of six bags, I think the donkeys could manage."

Finbar nodded. "So I run the *Holy Trinity* into the harbor here, pick up the money, and sail to Ireland. I know the very place, where I have bought armor and swords for trading before now."

"When do you think you could pick up the money?" Cormac asked.

Finbar thought for a moment. "It will take me a day and a bit to walk back to the ship," he calculated. "Then allow another day to sail round here, unless the weather does something extraordinary. Say in two nights' time. I think it would be unwise for me to anchor in the bay by daylight. At the very least it might make the soldiers curious. So I will come in at night. You will see the riding lights on my ship. Not many ships sail past here, as you will have noticed, and I would rather not give a signal unless I have to. But I will need to know that it is safe to come into the bay and drop anchor. The question is, how will I know?"

We all looked at one another. I had an idea. "What if we lit a fire on that ledge halfway down the cliff?" I said. "Provided the wind is not blowing onshore. It should not show too much, if at all, in the village, though maybe there would be a glow, I don't know. It would be all right so long as the soldiers were not paying us a visit."

"No fire, no dropping anchor," said Finbar, nodding. "But if I see the fire, I will sail into the harbor, and you can lead the donkeys down."

Wise Child suddenly spoke up. "How long will the trip to Ireland take?" she asked.

Finbar regarded her quietly for a moment, and I was reminded of all the time he had already spent away from her on his many voyages.

"Only a few days to get there," he said. "There will be swords, daggers, and pikes already for sale, but probably not enough, and we shall need helmets and breastplates of different sizes."

He paused, then regretfully said, "It will probably take at least a month for them to get the work done."

We were all a bit shocked by this, especially Wise Child, whose face seemed to close up. It was comforting to have Finbar around, and the thought of him leaving us for so long made us feel more vulnerable. But of course, there was no choice.

Attempting to lighten the mood, Finbar smiled at Wise Child and playfully asked, "So what will you do while I am gone?"

"Well, I have a plan," said Wise Child unexpectedly, "but I am not ready to talk about it yet."

Finbar suddenly looked uneasy.

"You won't do anything without telling anybody," he said.

"No, of course not," Wise Child said. "We're all together in this. I learned that yesterday. It's just that I want a bit more time in order to think about it and to learn some things."

Juniper eyed her thoughtfully but said nothing.

One of the things that Wise Child wanted to learn, I soon discovered, was to talk the Cornish language. Leaving Juniper, Finbar, and Cormac to their planning, Wise Child and I visited Lyon's house, where Wise Child pestered Lyon and his wife to repeat ordinary words to her.

On our way home I asked her, "Is learning Cornish to do with your secret plan?"

"It might be."

"Will you share the secret with me?"

"Very soon, I promise. I'm not keeping it from you just to be mean."

"Will I be part of it?"

"Yes, you will!" Her eyes gleamed as she said this.

"It is lovely to see you sort of more alive again," I said tentatively.

"I know," Wise Child said. "I felt so miserable I hardly knew what to do with myself, and now I don't. In fact, I feel full of energy."

Juniper called to us as we came in. Finbar suggested that we needed two alternative signals, one to say that it was safe, the other to warn him if the soldiers arrived in the middle of the operation.

"You are in charge of this, Colman," said Finbar. "The others have to get the gold down the cliff, but you will wait at the ledge to man the signal."

"Right!" I said. "If it is safe, I light the fire. If danger approaches, I will douse it."

"Better make sure you have plenty of fuel, then," said Finbar. "You don't want the fire to go out through lack of wood."

"Suppose it is a foggy night?" I asked. "There is often fog round here."

"If it is foggy, I shall have to leave and return later," said Finbar. "We cannot risk getting caught, though I don't feel the danger is great. I am going now to discuss it all with Lyon. The outlaws must approve what we are doing."

While Finbar was gone, Juniper tipped out some of the golden coins on the bedroom floor. Wise Child and I were absolutely entranced by them, picking them up and running them through our fingers.

We entertained ourselves until Finbar returned. The long meeting in the Cave of the Mermaids, the exchange of ideas between Juniper and Finbar and the outlaws, and the action of Wise Child, which had shown such a clear concern for their safety, had seemed to bring us much closer to the people of Castle Dore. There was no difficulty about borrowing the donkeys.

Finbar had Lyon with him. Lyon was obviously astonished, in spite of what Juniper had said the day before, that there were means to help pay for the weapons and armor the men needed.

"And there is more money if you need it," Juniper told him earnestly. "Would it be possible for you to buy food from other peoples nearby to help feed your families?"

He seemed doubtful of this, saying that they, too, were under the heel of the Gray Knight, but that in any case, it would be difficult to bring back large quantities of food—of meat or flour, say—without risk of being caught by Perquin's men and suffering terrible punishment as a result.

Lyon insisted on only one thing. Rather than having Finbar's men lower a boat from the *Holy Trinity* and come ashore, he felt that it would be better if one of Castle Dore's own small fishing boats put out from the harbor once the donkeys had got down there with the money.

"In the case of 'interruption,' it would make you less vulnerable," Lyon said. "Whatever happened, you could get away."

Finbar agreed, admitting that the local men knew the rocks of the cove as he and his men did not. And then Finbar was gone, and all of us were slightly subdued because of it.

To keep her spirits up, Wise Child started to play a game of finchnell against herself. She set out the pieces for two players and arranged a chair on each side of the table. After she made a move, she went and sat on the opposite chair and solemnly thought out how to counteract the first move.

"I am practicing being two people," she said when I finally asked her about it. "One of them is the kind of person who is determined to win at all costs. The other is a person who is totally indifferent to winning. I want to see who comes off best."

I noticed Juniper listening very hard to this conversation. "So who does come off best?" she asked.

"I'm not sure, because I sometimes forget which is which," Wise Child answered honestly. "Or rather both of them want to win, and I don't know how to make one of them indifferent. But I like trying."

So this strange game was going on in one corner of the royal apartments, while in another Cormac was repairing a pair of shoes. Juniper wandered down the passageway to Erlain's bedroom. After a moment I followed her and found her sitting absolutely silent and still in a way she had that made you think how much everyone else talked and fidgeted.

I sat down next to her, and after a bit I said, "So what about Euny and all the magic stuff? What's going to happen about that?"

At first I thought she was not going to reply, but then she said, "That comes later."

I had a nasty moment of foreboding.

"Will it be very dangerous?"

"At times, yes. But we have our protections and our own good sense."

"Could we be killed, or imprisoned?"

"I guess we could, but we shall try not to."

It was not very comforting, and yet I knew Juniper always spoke the truth.

Suddenly Wise Child called out, "I want to say something!"

Juniper and I sat and waited. Wise Child had always been good at a dramatic pause. Finally she came in and sat down on the far side of the room.

"I want to make a suggestion," she said. Something in her manner made me sense that she was a little nervous. Juniper said nothing.

"You remember," Wise Child said, "that you thought we needed to infiltrate Caerleon, partly to get the feel of what was going on there, partly to try to find out more about Prince Brangwyn? The Castle Dore people were unhappy about that. They said that nobody who went to Caerleon was allowed to return home, and they just did not want to go. And you and Finbar can't go, because Meroot might recognize you. It occurred to me then that I could go, with Cormac and Colman if they would agree; we could offer ourselves as servants. That way, no one would pay attention to us. We would count for nothing, and that would mean that we had all the more chance to observe. It would be obvious from our speech that we are not local people, though I think we should try to learn a bit of Cornish beforehand. Sooner or later we could try to smuggle information out, if necessary along the route that you told the outlaws about, which you and Finbar used to escape from the castle before."

I found myself watching Juniper's face as this speech went on. Allowing children to do dangerous things was one thing, but letting us go into the very stronghold of the enemy was quite another. I felt quite choky at the thought of it, and rather hoped that Juniper would say it was completely out of the question.

Instead she called to Cormac, "Could you come here a moment?" When he came, a shoe he was stitching still in his hand, she asked Wise Child to repeat what she had just said. Cormac's face reflected the astonishment I had felt myself. He sat down rather quickly and said, "That is a very bold idea, Wise Child."

Juniper fixed Wise Child with her beautiful, dark eyes and said, very earnestly, "Why are you suggesting this?"

Wise Child considered. "I suppose I just have a sense it would work," she said. "I agreed with you when you said it was one of the things that needed to be done. There is no one else to go—no one who sees the situation as we see it, I mean. We have the protections Colman found on the mountain, and somehow I feel that we are meant to succeed."

"Do you feel fear?" Juniper asked, maybe thinking of the Wise Child who had been terrorized by the trial and the escape.

"Yes, of course I do," said Wise Child. "The Gray Knight and Meroot are dangerous, cruel people. It's just that, well, you have taught me that the job of a *doran* is to take on people like them."

"When you are fully trained, grown-up, old enough to choose such risks for yourself," Juniper said softly.

"Perhaps it is not about age and training," said Wise Child, "but about willingness." She looked at Juniper with wide blue eyes that were not very childlike. She was a world away from the young girl who had just been playing with the finchnell pieces.

Wise Child and Juniper gazed at each other silently for a minute or two, and then Juniper got up and walked out of the room. Wise Child shrugged and went back to another game of finchnell. Cormac went back to repairing his shoe. It was as if the three of them had shelved the important question—or had Juniper ruled it out? I did not know. I sat alone, feeling disturbed. Entering Caerleon was a terrifying project, but I felt Wise Child meant what she said.

It was nearly dark by the time Juniper returned. Cormac, Wise Child, and I were preparing supper by then, and the four of us sat down at the table together.

"I'm appalled by what you said," Juniper said abruptly to Wise Child. "I think the risks are enormous, and although the protections will help, you and Colman are not knowledgeable about using them. Also, we would need to talk to Finbar."

"I purposely did not mention it while he was here," said Wise Child with a touch of her old crossness. "He'd be bound to forbid it."

"That was foolish of you. You could not do anything like that without his consent."

"Then it won't happen," said Wise Child. "He'll never agree."

"He might if I asked him," Juniper said softly.

We all stopped what we were doing and stared at Juniper in surprise.

"I would love to be able to say that you must not do it," she went on, "because the whole idea terrifies me. However, because the *doran* spirit is strong within you at the moment, I dare not forbid you, though I still hope you won't go. The spirit has its own energy, which you are clearly feeling, something that your actions the other day also suggested. In one sense, the fact that you are still a child is irrelevant. I also believe that Euny, and the Mother, will protect you. But oh, my darling Wise Child, I am also very frightened!"

Wise Child came to Juniper and put her arms round her, and Juniper picked her up, sat her on her lap, and rocked her. "My little girl!"

"What about Cormac and Colman?" Wise Child said after a bit.

Juniper raised her eyes at Cormac, who gave her his gentle, lopsided grin.

"Do you think I would let Wise Child run into danger if I could be there to help her?" he said.

Wise Child beamed at Cormac.

There was an awkward silence after all these feelings had been laid bare, and I felt the others were waiting for me to speak. I found it difficult to believe what I had been hearing. With all we knew about the wickedness of the Gray Knight and Meroot, it seemed madness to risk putting ourselves in their hands. It was like putting one's head into a lion's mouth! Juniper and Finbar had only just escaped with their lives at Caerleon many years before, and yet Juniper, *Juniper*, whose common sense and wisdom I had always revered, seemed to think that the scheme might be possible.

"I don't know," I heard myself saying reluctantly. "I am Wise Child's friend, and I hope I am not a coward, but this plan seems dangerous beyond belief. What if Meroot smells us out with her magical powers? We shall barely get across the doorstep!"

In the two days that followed, we went ahead with the tasks needed to get the gold onto Finbar's ship. Wise Child and I carried lots of wood down to the ledge—no easy task— and found an old blanket to cover it and keep it dry. We borrowed a tin cupboard from the kitchen of the royal apartments and put a tinderbox and a candle inside it. We also hid some oil, which we would use to start the fire. It seemed to me that fog apart, there would be a clear view of our signal from a ship at sea.

Lyon came up from the village with three donkeys and tied them outside his workshop. We checked that the bags of gold would slip easily into the donkeys' saddlebags.

By common consent we did not discuss Wise Child's daring project. I felt a sense of shame at my reluctance to participate and a slight coolness from Wise Child. This hurt, especially since I had enjoyed the renewed warmth of our friendship after the day she found her way through the tunnel.

In our minds we followed Finbar back to his ship, calculating where he had got to as he returned to the ship and then began his voyage along the coast. It was exciting. I realized that I liked the feeling of doing something a little daring, not least because the plan felt a manageable one.

On the afternoon of the second day, in the last of the daylight, Wise Child and I went to and fro carrying big jugs of water that in case of emergency I could use to douse the flames. Then, taking some of the wood we had stored, but leaving some more to keep the fire going, we carefully built our bonfire as a sort of pyramid. There was a hole in the side where I could wriggle in with a lighted candle and set light to some oil-soaked rags and twigs before getting out quickly so that the bigger sticks and branches would catch alight. The ledge was big enough for me to get quite a long way away from the fire, which I guessed might be very hot when it got going properly.

From about midnight I stayed on the ledge, wearing all the warm clothes I had been able to fit onto myself at the royal apartments. Huddled among the rocks, I was out of the worst of the cold, but whenever I ventured onto the cliff, it was very cold indeed. There was no fog that I could see, which was a relief, and no rain, but it was windy, which would make the fire catch but also might make it hard to control.

A little later Cormac appeared and said that they were about to take the donkeys down to the cove. If by any chance Finbar did not show, they would simply come back again, and we would return the next night. There was no sight or sound of any soldiers, so we hoped the mission could be safely achieved—though I noticed that the moon was nearly full and cast a great deal of light. If the soldiers wanted to make a nighttime visit, this night would be ideal.

My eyes continually scanned the sea for sight of Finbar's ship. And then—was I imagining things? Yes, no, yes . . . his riding lights were really there! With shaking hands, I opened the tinderbox, worked away with the flint, and lit the candle (I had already practiced this a few times), placing my body between it and the wind, though it still flickered alarmingly. Then I climbed into the fire according to plan and put the candle to the twigs and some of the oil-soaked cloths we had used. The flames caught quite quickly, setting the twigs alight, and then, more slowly, the sticks above them, and finally the branches. As I drew away from the fire, our signal shone out bravely into the night!

I could see nothing of what went on down below—

whether a boat had already put out for Finbar's ship—but I waited patiently, knowing that I would know nothing until the party returned. I felt triumphant. At this very moment the men were probably heaving the gold onto Finbar's ship. For a little while I felt very happy.

Then suddenly, unbelievably, I heard the jingle of harness and the calling out of orders. It came from far away, carried on the wind, so much so that for a moment I doubted whether I had heard it at all. But every time I decided I had made it up, the sound returned. I groaned aloud.

I did not fear that I would be caught, or seen, up on the cliff. The footing was too dangerous for horses in the dark, and the signal faced outward and could probably not be seen inland. But the others . . .

Even as I listened I could heard the sound of hooves and harness moving down in the direction of the harbor. In desperation I snatched up one of the jugs and began to pour water wildly over the fire. The first jug seemed not to make much difference, but after I had poured the second one, the fire quickly died down, and at the third jug the fire was nearly doused. My fear was that with the all-clear signal having already reached them, Finbar and his men might have given up watching the light and be concentrating on the arrival of the boat.

Yet, was it my imagination, or did I hear a cry from the *Trinity*? I was not sure. Cold as it was up there on the cliff, I found myself sweating in fear as I thought of Juniper, Cormac, Wise Child, and Lyon and his men falling into appalling danger.

When I had put out the fire, I noticed that Finbar's ship had pulled anchor and was sailing out into the bay. Should I go down to the harbor? No, it would not help if I ran into the soldiers and got myself arrested. I made quite sure the fire was extinguished, stamped on the last embers, hid the cupboard among the rocks, and headed back to the royal apartments with a heavy heart. Once inside, I locked the door and went to bed, lying there unsleeping in an agony of mind as I imagined all of the others arrested, to suffer God knew what fate at the hands of Perquin or the Gray Knight.

The time went slowly by, and I tried to work out what was the next thing for me to do—to talk to Lyon's wife, perhaps. Suddenly I heard a tapping on the door, and I got up and crept toward it. The handle turned as it had done before, but the gentle tapping, which continued, did not seem to be the way that soldiers would knock. I got close to the door and listened and to my huge relief heard the complaining voice of Wise Child.

"I do wish he'd hurry up. I'm frozen!"

I threw open the door. Outside stood Juniper, Wise Child, and Cormac.

"What happened? What happened?" I shouted at them. I felt a sudden anger after all the fear and distress I had known.

"It's all right, Colman," Juniper said. "Nothing happened, except that Finbar collected the money from us and sailed safely away."

"But when the soldiers arrived, what did you do?" I was still shouting as if my feelings of relief were bursting out of me.

"When we reached Finbar's ship, one of his men noticed that your signal had changed, and therefore we knew something was wrong. We did not go back to the harbor. There is a sea entrance to the Cave of the Mermaids, and we sailed into it and anchored the boat there. We had to wait for a while in case the soldiers were waiting for us somewhere, but since we were using no lights, we don't believe the soldiers even knew we were there. Eventually we left the boat in the cave and came back here on foot."

Suddenly, to my embarrassment, I started to cry.

"I thought I had lost you all," I said, doing my unsuccessful best to stop my lips from trembling and brushing the tears out of my eyes.

"It must have been awful for you," Juniper said kindly. "But how lucky you heard the soldiers and changed the signal. You saved us!"

"Lyon got back all right, then?" I asked gruffly, trying to pull myself together.

"Yes, everyone's fine. All in all, a successful evening."

Just as I was dropping off to sleep, something occurred to me.

"What happened to the donkeys?" I asked.

"We took off their saddles and let them wander on the beach," Wise Child replied sleepily. "You know what donkeys are for wandering. No one would think anything of it."

CHAPTER SIX

E ver since the day when she found the way down to the cave, Wise Child had continued to wear the silver crescent moon on its leather thong that the Mother had given to me in the hut on the mountain. Neither of us mentioned it. I had a feeling that that was the way I wanted it, that I felt better when I was not wearing it, and since Wise Child was happy to do so, it seemed a good arrangement. It was Juniper, of course, sharp-eyed as always, who commented on it.

"You seem to have given the amulet to Wise Child to wear," she said to me when we were alone one day. "Why is that?"

I was not sure that I knew the reason, or at any rate could put it into words, so I shrugged and said nothing.

"It was given to you," Juniper pointed out.

"Maybe," I said. "Or maybe the Mother gave it to me so that I could give it to Wise Child."

Juniper gave me a hard look, trying to understand what I meant. Suddenly I could not bear the questioning, and I got quite angry, something that had never happened between me and Juniper before.

"Leave me alone!" I shouted. Juniper nodded, not at all put out, and, taking me literally, immediately walked away. I felt upset and miserable but did not really understand why.

The day came when Wise Child and I, shepherded by Lyon and Merrion and wearing some clothes lent us by local families to make us less conspicuous, went with the people of Castle Dore to hear Perquin give his speech. We sat with the other children on a large grassy expanse that, in happier days, had been used for games of wrestling and horsemanship. The ground rose slightly upward, forming a natural stage slightly above the field itself, and it was there that Perquin would stand to address us. Behind him, towering above, were the charred remains of the great Wooden Palace, a chilling and horrible reminder of what the proud people of Castle Dore had been reduced to. As they listened to him, they would be forced to look at this sad spectacle, something no doubt planned by Meroot and the Gray Knight.

I had been curious to see Perquin, about whom so many stories were told. I had somehow assumed he would be tall and powerful-looking, but he was small and walked in heeled shoes with an odd sort of strut, as if trying to convey his own importance. He was also overdressed in a colored silken suit of rather garish colors and a cloak that made him look smaller and which he flourished around him as he walked in a way that was laughable. Only nobody laughed.

We knew from Lyon that Perquin used these occasions to harangue and intimidate the people, but that his speeches often contained some hint of his suspicions and that this was a useful way of discovering whether he suspected any plots.

"I am commanded," he began pompously, "by the high lord of Caerleon, the Gray Knight, and his wife, the Lady Meroot, to pay this visit to his people of Castle Dore, to ensure that they are behaving in perfect obedience to his noble decrees, that they are acting with the subservience appropriate to a subject people, and that they are yielding up whatever tithes of crops and herds his lordship may choose to demand. Long live the Gray Knight!"

The soldiers moved among the people, exhorting them to cheer, and a faint sound, almost like a sigh, emerged from them. A look of displeasure crossed Perquin's face.

"May I remind you," he said nastily, "that you continue to live only by the mercy of the high lord of Caerleon. You are in his power; it is he who allows you to live, though if he wished he could crush you like ants under his feet."

Perquin's face twisted with cruelty as he spoke, and I heard Wise Child give a soft little sound beside me, a kind of growl.

"I am sent here," he continued, "to tell you to attempt no violence against the forces of Caerleon, to seek no allies to support you, to do nothing but simply obey the decrees that the high lord of Caerleon lays down. You are his slaves, his underlings, as you and your children will always be. The might of Castle Dore, the legacy of King Mark, has been destroyed, and all its beauty laid waste. It will never return in your lifetime, or the lifetime of your children or children's children or their descendants. It has been wiped out forever. Do not sing the songs or tell the stories of that time, for you are now nothing."

Perquin's voice sank to a low, spiteful tone on the last word. He was a powerful speaker in spite of his foolish clothes and his tiny stature, and we could feel a shiver of dread run through the people. It was horrible to see.

"One more thing, and then you are dismissed back to the hovels in which you live. The high lord has decided that he has been forbearing with you for too long. He demands another three hundred bushels of wheat from you at harvest time and another hundred sheep a year from your flocks. Long live the Gray Knight!"

Another ragged cheer went up from the people as they turned away, their faces stricken at the further tribute the Gray Knight was demanding from their limited resources. I shall never forget their beaten look as, without a word, they left the field, hurried along quite unnecessarily by the soldiers.

"One good thing," Lyon said as we neared the royal apartments. "I don't think Perquin has got wind of any of our plans. His warnings are always more pointed than they were today if he thinks some plot is afoot."

He and Merrion left us at the royal apartments without a word, and we went in to find Juniper and Cormac there.

Wise Child did not wait for questions.

"That settles it, as far as I am concerned," she said. "Whatever it takes to get rid of those horrible people and restore Castle Dore to its former glory, I intend to do!"

Juniper shook her head. "The more I think about it, the more I think that you are not old enough to take those sorts of risks," she said firmly.

Wise Child stared very hard at Juniper, and there was a look on her face that I had never seen before. It was not a child's look. It might have been the expression of someone years older.

"You are training me as a *doran*," she said at last. "As I understand it, to be a *doran* makes demands that must be obeyed."

"That is true," said Juniper. "There are laws in the world to which *dorans* are particularly sensitive, and it is their job to obey those laws and use their skills to bring about harmony in the world."

"Exactly!" said Wise Child. "And that is what I am proposing to do. You need someone to infiltrate Caerleon. I have at least some of the skills, and I am offering to do so."

"You may be a *doran* in the making, but you are also a child."

"How old were you went you went to Caerleon and challenged the might of the Gray Knight and Meroot?" Wise Child asked.

I could see that Juniper was slightly shaken by this.

"Two or three years older than you."

"The time brings forth the deed," Wise Child declared. I knew this was a quotation from one of the epic songs Juniper and Wise Child used to sing together.

A silence, and not a very comfortable one, fell between them.

"Anyway," Wise Child went on, suddenly sounding much more childish, "Colman would come with me."

"I have not heard him say so," Juniper said.

"Would you?" Wise Child asked me directly.

I had been dreading this moment, but now that it was here, I knew that just because Wise Child's plan was brave, indeed heroic, it did not mean that it was the right thing to do.

"I cannot quite see what it would achieve," I said at last, knowing that I was betraying Wise Child.

Wise Child gave a sound of annoyance like "Tcha!" and turned to Cormac, who had been sitting silently, as usual.

"You'd come with me, wouldn't you, Cormac?" she said.

Cormac nodded. "I have said I would, and I will. *Someone* needs to penetrate the stronghold of Caerleon; Juniper is right about that, so why not us? Between Wise Child's magical skills and my grown-upness, for what it's worth, I think we could manage it and learn vital information about Prince Brangwyn."

Wise Child looked at Cormac in triumph, and Juniper was suddenly crestfallen.

"I think you are underestimating her," said Cormac gently to Juniper.

Juniper sat very still, obviously struggling with contradictory thoughts. Wise Child was, at least by adoption, her little girl. How could she let her run into such horrible danger? On the other hand, Wise Child was also her student, the one she was training as a *doran*. It was precisely for such confrontations between good and evil that the *dorans* were trained. Was her caution a mistake, a refusal to allow a healing act to take place?

Juniper reached for her cloak, put it on without a word, and went out. Wise Child sat for a while staring in front of her.

"I will play a game of finchnell with you if you like," I said, wanting to show her that to some degree I was still on her side.

"I don't think so!" she said scornfully. "I'd rather play against myself."

Miserable, I slunk off to the bedroom, climbed into

113

bed, and pulled the covers over my head. Sometimes life was too complicated to get right. Even loving other people didn't necessarily help you; it could just make things worse.

I don't know how long I lay there, dozing some of the time and some of the time awake, when I heard Wise Child's and Juniper's voices in the big room and realized that another stage in their argument was beginning.

"I've got an idea," Wise Child said loudly. (She often did talk loudly when she got excited.) "What you really need to know is whether this is some harebrained scheme of mine that would run me and Cormac into danger or whether it comes from some . . . deeper level, some bit of me that knows what has to be done. Let me say that as soon as I heard you mention that someone needed to infiltrate Caerleon, I felt a certainty that I was the right person. No one but myself can know for certain that I have that sense of conviction, I quite see. Isn't this, therefore, time to use one of the *doran* insights—scrying, talking to a wise animal, flying, fasting, whatever you think—to see whether I might be right?"

I had got out of bed by now and was standing in the doorway looking at these two beloved people as they struggled with their disagreement. A look of acute pain crossed Juniper's face.

"I think that I may be allowing my love for you to cloud my judgment," she said humbly. "But I cannot bear to think of you at Caerleon."

"I understand that," replied Wise Child, almost as one grown-up to another, in a tone of voice that struck me as both sympathetic toward Juniper's feelings and yet ruthless in her sense of what she must do. "*That* is why I am suggesting a different way of coming at the problem."

"The dreaming bundle," Juniper said suddenly.

"What?"

"Do you remember the bundle of twigs with leaves that Colman found at the door of the Mother's hut? How I couldn't think quite what they were? I have just remembered. They are what is known as a 'dreaming bundle.' You make tea with an infusion of the leaves, you drink it, you dream, and if all goes well, the dream tells you what you want to know. What is interesting about a gift like that from the Mother is that it is quite specific. You are given what is necessary to solve the particular problems in front of you—no more and no less—though it is up to you to use the gifts intelligently and thoughtfully. And if ever we needed insight, it is now."

Wise Child seemed slightly stunned by what Juniper had said.

"You mean you are going to do it? Make the tea, drink it, dream, and see what you come up with?"

"Yes, but not just me. You, Cormac, and Colman, if he wants to."

"And you will abide by what the dreams say?"

"Of course. Why do it else?"

Wise Child sat down suddenly, as if all the energy had gone out of her. She had been so sure of Juniper's opposition, so full of arguments, and now there was no need of them. As often happened to all of us with Juniper, Wise Child was taken by surprise.

"I'm not going to do all the work, though," Juniper said. "The leaves need to be gently crumbled for a start. We'd better get on with it."

"So when will we drink it?" Wise Child asked.

"Late this afternoon," said Juniper. "It takes a little while to work. By the time we go to bed, we should be ready to dream, and tomorrow we shall share our discoveries."

Wise Child kept staring at Juniper as if she could not believe what she was hearing, but she said no more and set to work preparing the tea from the dreaming bundle.

It was a lovely spring day, and I went out to sit by myself on the cliff. I did not much like the sound of the dreaming process, and I dreaded the implications if the results were positive. I wished Finbar were still around. I realized how much I had enjoyed his company and somehow could not imagine him going along with what was happening. I suddenly had a rare pang of homesickness—I could see our cottage full of children, usually with washing hanging up to dry in front of the fire, and I longed to be back safely inside it, even if Dad would be coming home at the end of the day.

We drank the tea in the late afternoon. Wise Child

and Juniper had crumbled all the leaves, boiled water, and steeped the leaves in it. It filled the royal apartments with a rather nice smell. Juniper laid out four goblets on the table and filled them one by one. She handed one goblet ceremonially to Wise Child, another to Cormac, and turned to me with the third.

"Do you want to, Colman?" she asked.

If she had not asked, I would probably have been too much of a coward to refuse, but since she had asked me, I found myself unable to say yes. I did not want to have a dream about the future! I shook my head, unable to speak.

"Very well!" said Juniper. She took up the third cup herself without further comment. No one said anything about my refusal, not even Wise Child.

They all took a sip. "Interesting taste!" Cormac remarked.

"I've never used a dreaming bundle before," Juniper said. "It never came my way, but it has quite a reputation for its accuracy."

Wise Child sipped the liquid slowly, with great concentration, her eyes big over the top of the goblet. She seemed far away in her thoughts.

"One thing you can do," Juniper went on, "is to ask a question that you want the dream to answer and go to sleep with that in your mind. Alternatively, you can ask the dream to take you where it wills. That has a slightly different outcome, I am told."

Cormac listened carefully to this as he drank his tea.

Wise Child seemed in a world of her own, as if the drink had already transported her. No one, it seemed, wanted any supper. Well, I did, so I went and foraged for myself in the kitchen. One by one they all crept off very early to bed until I was the only wakeful person in the house. And not a very happy person at that.

Eventually I, too, went to bed. Wise Child was sleeping very peacefully—if she was already dreaming, it did not show—but I tossed and turned for a long time. Finally I fell into an uneasy sleep and dreamed that Dad was about to come home and that I was in trouble.

When I woke the next morning, there was no sign of Wise Child—sometimes now she liked to get up early and go out for a walk on the cliff. Cormac and Juniper were both still asleep, and I awaited with some curiosity the outcome of the tea.

I was beginning to prepare breakfast when Wise Child returned. She looked at me a little shiftily, I thought, and immediately went off by herself into the bedroom with hardly a word.

Finally, however, Cormac and Juniper got up, both of them sleepy, and we ate a silent breakfast together. Nobody, it seemed, wanted to be the first to raise the question of dreams.

It was Juniper who brought the subject up eventually.

"Well, it worked," she said. "I dreamed, all right. Bits of it have a pretty clear meaning, though other parts are harder to make sense of."

She had the undivided attention of all three of us.

"I dreamed that I was in the Mother's hut with Euny," Juniper went on. "Euny took the Mother's baby and handed it to me. 'It is yours!' she said, and I took it and held it in my arms. I carried it all the way to Caerleon, and there I laid it down upon the doorstep and left it."

There was a catch in Juniper's voice as she said this.

"Why?" Wise Child asked her.

"Because that was what Euny had said I must do, with the words 'She will be taken care of.'"

"Did you mind?"

"Very much. There was also a bit—a later sequence—when Castle Dore shone like gold. It was still burned and ruined, yet it was amazingly beautiful, and it was full of people who were singing. The joy was indescribable."

Juniper's words left a silence behind them. We could think of nothing to say.

After a long pause, as if waiting to be sure that Juniper had finished, Cormac said, "My dream took place inside Caerleon. It felt very sinister. There were whisperings in corners and things half seen out of the corner of the eye and the feeling that I was being watched through holes in the tapestry. The sense of power around me was crushing—it would be useless to resist. Then there was a will o' the wisp, a tiny fragment of light that danced over the walls and the ceiling, and it made Meroot very cross, only she could not work out where it was coming from. It was free—that was what she did not like about it. Wise Child was there, and

Colman, and some other children, and they were trying not
to giggle.

"There was another scene, too, that was about the
Gray Knight. He was a dog part of the time, only it was
very odd. It was as if he was wearing a disguise that kept
slipping, and I could suddenly see a bit of gray silk breeches
on the dog's flank or a human nose on its face, and then,
just as if he was making a tremendous effort, it would
return to a dog's leg or a dog's face."

Again there was silence as we tried to take in the
meaning of the dream. Juniper turned to Wise Child.

"I can't remember anything," Wise Child said desperately. "I don't even know whether I dreamed or not."

She suddenly looked like a much younger child.

"It's because you are trying too hard," Juniper told
her. "Just let it come."

We waited, but nothing came. Juniper suddenly
started.

"Well, I've just remembered a bit more of my
dream," she said. "Wise Child and I were sitting out on the
steps at the white house, the way we often did on summer
evenings. We were laughing together, were in fits of gig-
gles, when Wise Child suddenly said to me, entirely
solemnly, 'The great question is unsolved.'"

Wise Child stirred at that. "I had been thinking of
those steps," she said, "and of how, I think on my second
day with you, I sat there with you and suddenly knew I was

safe, that I could trust you, that I had found my home. We giggled a lot that day, too."

She paused, and a strange look came over her face, so that it was almost as if she was in a trance.

"I do remember my dream—well, almost. I am wearing a mask, but it is one that everyone takes for my real face, and I am almost not quite sure that it is not the real me. But then I finger a talisman Juniper once gave me, which is in my pocket, and I know that my life with Juniper is the real me and that I must carry this with me, mask or no mask. Later the mask is gone. I am beautifully dressed, and I am dancing. Colman is with me, but what is important is that I am taking on some of the power of the *doran*. It frightens me, I know it is risky, but it is also what I long to do. Then I am back at Castle Dore. It is in moonlight, looking very beautiful, though still ruined, but Prince Brangwyn is there and he says to me, 'There is no loss. All is gain.'" She hesitated. "There was more, but I cannot reach the rest of it."

Juniper nodded decisively. "There seems little doubt that Wise Child, Cormac, and Colman are going to Caerleon," she said. "My dream is in part about what I feared most, letting Wise Child run horrible risks when I am not there to help her. Yet the dream seems to promise a happy outcome."

"You have already lost so much," said Cormac, "and now you have to run a greater risk."

"I know," said Juniper.

"My dream is mainly about fear," Cormac went on. "The sheer darkness and horror of a place where there is no love, only cruelty. The bit about the dog, though, might suggest that the Gray Knight is not as all-powerful as he tries to pretend."

"*My* dream," said Wise Child, "is saying that though I must pretend at Caerleon, I will succeed by holding on to the truest part of me, the part that loves Juniper. And also that if power comes, I must not be afraid of it. Will I be afraid of it?"

"Power is very frightening," said Juniper, "especially if you are not used to it. The danger is that it may take you over and control you entirely. Some people are so scared of it that they will not take it in any form at all."

"Is that good?"

"It is really harmful," Juniper said. "If the good people, or those who at least try to be good, will not take their power, it leaves it all to the bad people, like Meroot, who can never get enough of it and want to use it for their own gratification. So, though power is dangerous to all of us, we have to learn how to take it when it comes our way and use it wisely and carefully. And unselfishly. That is the difficult bit."

"I'd never thought of all that," said Wise Child. "I thought power might be rather exciting."

"It is that, too," said Juniper. "There lies the risk. You can get drunk on it. You have to learn how to manage it, as one day you will learn how to drink wine without getting drunk."

"So I may go to Caerleon, using whatever power I have, and do it with your blessing?" Wise Child asked, returning to the main purpose of the dreaming.

Juniper nodded slowly, painfully. A tear rolled down her cheek. Cormac put out a hand and laid it over Juniper's.

"I will take what care of her I can," he said gently.

"We will need to let Lyon know and get the outlaws' permission," Wise Child said.

"I have already done so," Juniper said.

I realized then that when Juniper had left earlier, she had not only been upset but had also gone to consult with the outlaws.

"Tell me, Cormac," Juniper said, "how it was that even before the dreaming, you were so sure that it was right for Wise Child to go? You know how much trust I have in you, how wise I have always believed you to be. In this matter you could see what I could not."

"When Wise Child talked as she did after Perquin's meeting, it was as if I could see what she saw, that she was called, called as a *doran,* to take some direct action against the evil of Caerleon. True, she is still a young girl, and the risks are very real, but it was as if the vocation of the *doran* was an ageless one, and suddenly I saw her not only as a child but also as a person called to a particular task, regardless of her age."

Juniper nodded again.

"So I must let her go?" she asked Cormac humbly.

"I think so," he replied.

"So when can I start?" Wise Child asked, suddenly much more the impatient child than the wise woman in the making.

"We need a few days to prepare you all," Juniper said. "Clothes, directions, and in Wise Child's case, magical lore, which will involve some learning by heart, as well as just generally thinking and talking through the various potential dangers for all three of you."

I surprised myself by suddenly saying, clearly and distinctly, "I am not going."

The other three stared at me.

"I am not going," I said again, very red in the face. "It is madness to go to Caerleon, and I don't want to be part of it, no matter what your dreams say."

Juniper looked at me so lovingly that I thought I might burst into tears. Cormac looked at me in surprise, and Wise Child with contempt.

"Then we'll do it without you," she said sharply.

It was three days later that they left, and they were three painful days for me, in which Wise Child barely spoke to me. At the first opportunity Juniper took me aside.

"You are sure about this, Colman? It seems"—she hesitated as she sought the words she needed—"unlike you."

I shook my head but said nothing. I felt very sad, as if I would never be happy again.

They set off early in the morning. With a heavy heart, I got up to see them go. Cormac clasped me warmly to him. Wise Child looked at me in her cool, slightly scornful way. The two of them put on their warm outdoor clothes and their strongest boots. Each of them carried, strapped to their backs, a bundle of clothes, which I knew included the black egg that the Mother had given to me, the flask of purple liquid, and the little bottle with the scrap of cloth inside it.

Juniper embraced Wise Child as if she could not bear to let her go, and both of them wept a little. Then they were gone.

CHAPTER SEVEN

In the days when Juniper lived on the island, she had always seemed confident, strong, and serene. She lived in her white house, she grew her herbs and harvested them, and she worked as a healer. Then, when Wise Child came to live with her, she also cared for her.

On Finbar's boat I had been shocked to see her ill and distressed, grieved at the loss of her home and life on the island. Since that voyage, life had dealt her other blows, including learning of her parents' deaths and the horror of seeing her beloved Castle Dore destroyed. Now, finally, she had relinquished Wise Child, knowing very well the dangers to which she would be exposed.

She looked thin and tired, and more than once as if she had been crying. I did not feel that I could mention this, and I had no idea how to cheer her up. Wise Child had told me once how, when she realized that Maeve, her mother, was never going to love her, she had made the decision that in the future Juniper would be her mother. It was clear to me that Juniper had responded completely to that wish and that it was now as if Wise Child was truly her own child. No wonder she was in anguish. I also wondered what she felt about the fact that I had more or less abandoned Wise Child. She did not mention my refusal to go to Caerleon.

I was in some anguish myself. Cormac would look after Wise Child as well as anyone could, but Wise Child had clearly counted on me to be part of the adventure. She was my best friend, and I had refused her request to accompany her. Of course, I had many good reasons for doing so. Still, I could not escape the knowledge that I had quite simply been afraid. I crept about the apartments feeling ashamed of myself.

Several days passed in which Juniper and I talked very little, though at times I caught a glimpse of the old Juniper. I would notice her regarding me with a quizzical look that gave me the feeling she could see right through me. We prepared our simple meals, went for walks on the cliff, and talked with Lyon and Merrion, who shared our worries for Wise Child and Cormac.

One morning I noticed a sudden change in Juniper. She seemed brighter, readier to talk to me, and over breakfast I discovered why.

"I have decided that I need to go to the Mother's hut myself," she said. "For one thing, I need to see whether I can get some clue about Euny—her help would be invaluable, if indeed she is still alive. I need some help to see how

I can best use my skills. I feel helpless here, and as I said to Finbar, the skill of the *dorans*—Wise Child and myself—may be as important as arms, indeed more important, in saving Castle Dore. I want to be sure to be back here by the time Finbar returns, so it seems best to set off at once. Since I cannot leave you here alone, I suggest you come with me."

I nodded, taking in all that she had said.

"There is something I want to ask you about, though," she said. "When you came back from the Mother's hut with the tokens and wearing the silver moon, not to mention when you were able to do the scrying in Ireland, it seemed to me that you, like Wise Child, might be a future *doran*. But more recently, I may be wrong, but I have felt that that might not be your wish after all."

I shifted uneasily in my seat. I did not want to hurt Juniper's feelings. She had been very good to me over the years, and I loved and cared for her as all her friends did.

"I can't explain," I said. "I suppose I *could* be a *doran* and that was why I was able to do the scrying and why the Mother gave me the gifts, but somehow it all makes me uneasy. It feels creepy to me, dealing with that magic stuff. Don't be angry with me—it seems rather rude—but what I would like best is for life just to be ordinary. I don't want to cast spells or do magical things. All that stuff about power really frightens me. It would make me feel lonely, because most people aren't like that. I would rather be something normal, like a farmer or a sailor."

I could see at once that Juniper was not angry at all and that she did not think that I was rude. She gave me a very loving smile and said that no one *had* to be a *doran*. There were many reasons for refusing. In fact, it was only if you felt that you *had* to be one that you should accept the vocation. At once I felt hugely relieved.

I surprised myself by saying, "I feel I could be more useful in helping Wise Child to become a *doran* than being one myself."

A silence fell between us in which it was obvious that we were both thinking about how, despite what I had just said, I had not been prepared to help Wise Child on her trip to Caerleon. Juniper's clear, candid eyes upon me made any sort of pretense impossible.

"It was true that I thought going to Caerleon a crazy idea," I blurted out. "But what stopped me, because after all Wise Child's crazy ideas often do work out, was that I was scared, terrified. I'm not proud of it."

"But you are brave enough to tell me," Juniper said gently.

"I'm a coward," I said wretchedly.

"You have never struck me like that," she said. "In fact, I would bet anything on your courage."

"But I let my best friend down."

Juniper made no comment, just digested what I had said and left me with it, which was a way she had.

I moved restlessly. "So what now?"

"You can come with me in search of Euny."

"You don't really need me. It doesn't feel quite right, but I don't know what does."

"I don't think I could leave you here alone. Although we have been safe so far, the soldiers might find out about us at any time. I suppose I could ask Lyon to take care of you. . . ." But her voice sounded doubtful. Our neighbors had enough problems of their own.

"When will you go?" I asked her.

"I thought tomorrow, or the next day at the latest."

A worrying thought stirred within me, one too frightening to share, even with Juniper.

"Not Lyon, I think," was all I said, and once again I could see Juniper's thoughtful gaze upon me.

"As you wish."

It was a moonlit night, and in the middle of it, not sleeping, I got up from bed, picked up the pack I had prepared earlier, and, moving as quietly as I could, dressed myself and got ready to go out. I had picked up the tablet and stylus earlier that day and before I went to bed had written on it my farewell to Juniper and told her what I proposed to do, with a message of love and good wishes in her search for Euny. I propped it up on the table where we ate so that she would find it first thing.

Then I silently let myself out of the royal apartments. I went on my way, past the ruin of Castle Dore, illuminated so brilliantly in the moonlight that it looked almost like its old self, and out onto the road. There I listened for approaching hooves in case the soldiers patrolled it and would catch a small boy breaking curfew. I knew that I must be well away from Castle Dore by daybreak, out in the open countryside, where I was unlikely to meet or be challenged by anyone. I had a good supply of food and drink, but it weighed heavy, along with my clothes, and I longed for the time when the pack would be lighter. But I could not afford to stop for many hours yet on my three-day walk to Caerleon. What a fool I had been!

I had no desire for sleep, just a burning desire to keep going, to reach my goal, which felt interminably far away. It was a sort of penance for my wrongdoing, one that I had to bear with fortitude.

I will not describe to you every stage of my journey. Indeed, I cannot remember all of it. I do remember that, hungry, thirsty, and tired after walking all night, I stopped in the middle of the morning in a small wood, devoured some bread and water, and fell asleep. To my horror I slept far longer than I intended, and the sun was already farther down in the sky than I liked when I woke up and set off again. My feet were sore to start with but seemed to ease into the walking. I tried hard to carry in my head all the directions Juniper had told to Wise Child and Cormac, but I did not have Wise Child's uncanny ability at finding the way. It was a great relief to see a house I remembered

Juniper mentioning, surrounded by a copse of conifer trees, just as she had described.

The days went on, and I trudged through them with a heavy heart. I brooded on many things as I walked—on what Juniper had thought when she received my message, on how Wise Child and Cormac were faring at Caerleon, on where Euny had gone and whether she was still alive, as Juniper seemed to believe. I found comfort in the memory of the Mother's hut and how safe and happy I had felt there.

Eventually, my supplies of food nearly gone, my feet so sore that I wished I need never take another step, I saw what I anticipated with dread—the towers of Castle Caerleon in the distance. It was still a long way off—it would take every ounce of my determination to finish the journey—but at least I would not now lose my way. Soon, with any luck, I would see Wise Child and Cormac again.

As I approached the side of Caerleon that led to the kitchens, wondering how on earth I would make myself understood there, an incredible thing happened. Several young women were working in the yard outside, one of them sweeping a carpet, another hanging out some washing. But there, standing at a well and filling buckets with water, was Wise Child. She looked up, stared, looked and looked again, and with a face full of astonishment said, "Colman!"

"I had to come," I said simply. "I felt ashamed. I thought you might need me."

"What did Juniper say?"

"I didn't tell her—I just got up in the night and left. Only I think she may have known I meant to do it. You know how she knows everything."

A silence fell between us. We were shy of each other. To hide my feelings I said, "So what's it like?"

"All right where I am, scrubbing away and doing all the dirty work in the sculleries. It's the hardest work ever. To think I used to tell Juniper that I didn't like doing housework. I had no idea! The language thing is difficult, but I am learning fast."

"But what about . . . you know"—I dropped my voice—"all the rest of it?"

Wise Child glanced quickly around, though of course no one would understand our language.

"I don't really see *them*, or only in the distance. Nor Juniper's brother." I felt she deliberately avoided his title in case it was recognizable in Cornish.

"And Cormac?"

"He's got a job as a sort of under-footman. I don't see all that much of him, either. Just by accident sometimes, or in the evenings."

"Will I be able to get a job?"

"I am sure you will. They always need scullery boys and workers. It's such a huge place. Let me just finish this, and I'll take you in and ask about it." I wanted to help her in with the heavy buckets, but she would not let me. She

133

took me into a room where an older lady sat at a table, clearly presiding over the kitchen workers.

In what sounded to me like fluent Cornish, Wise Child introduced me to her—her name was Dame Vawn—and then translated back her response, which was that she could employ me in the scullery. Rather briskly, she got up from the table and hustled me down to the bowels of the kitchen, where one of the cooks at once set me to work washing a pile of greasy plates. I heaved a sigh of relief. Tired as I was, I had made it safely into Caerleon. Troubles, I knew, lay ahead, but for the time being I could relax, knowing that I had done what I must and had put things right between Wise Child and myself.

I did not see her again until late in the afternoon, when many of the kitchen workers had a rather paltry meal together.

"The food here isn't much for people who have to work so hard," Wise Child said to me. "They are mean with it."

But I was so hungry that the gruel, and even the thin ale that accompanied it, was very welcome to me. I was soon yawning—I had a lot of sleep I needed to make up—and I discovered that the scullery boys put down mats in a dingy, airless room near the kitchens. With only a blanket or two each and a meager pillow, they got what sleep they could. That first night, however, the discomfort did not bother me.

We were awakened at dawn the next day—just when I was desperate for more sleep—and driven out to wash our faces under the pump in the yard. Then we were put to work running errands for the cooks. I was kept racing around for most of the morning, shouted at by the cooks, who all seemed to be bad-tempered. By noon I was exhausted. After that things seemed to calm down a bit, and I sat with Wise Child and ate some black bread with goose grease on it, an onion or two with a kind of pickle, and water from the well.

"It's so good you are here!" she exclaimed suddenly, and I could think of nothing to say in reply beyond a nod of agreement. I could have spent hours describing the feelings I had had, and it did not seem worth starting. Perhaps one day I would say more.

But one thing I had to ask.

"I don't see how it is going to work," I said. "You and me stuck in the kitchens, Cormac somewhere else in the house. What difference is it going to make to Castle Dore or the prince or anyone?"

Wise Child's face set in its firmest expression.

"I know that it will. Take my word for it. Here we are, sort of invisible, just like all the other workers, but we have a purpose, and sooner or later we shall get the chance to work on it. We just have to wait for the opportunity."

I felt a bit doubtful. It seemed to me that we might go on working indefinitely in the kitchens and have no chance either to find anything out or to make the slightest difference to the fate of anyone. But I was tired by my morning's work and not looking forward much to other days that would be equally hard.

"You know," said Wise Child, returning to her original theme, "it means a lot to me to have you here. I *knew* you would come, and I was baffled when you refused. I *saw* you here. Cormac, too."

It was hard to argue with that.

"All the same," I said grumpily, "I hope something else happens soon."

Wise Child laughed, as she often did when I was cross.

"Wait and see," she said.

The days began to pass and nothing very much did happen. I saw Cormac once or twice when he was sent down to the kitchen with a message. He was more surprised to see me than Wise Child had been. We slipped together behind a door into a pantry and had a brief conversation. After I had explained to him, a bit shamefacedly, how I had decided to come to Caerleon after all, I asked him whether he saw any opportunity for us to take action. He looked me full in the face and said, "Colman, it is an odd thing for a grown-up to say, but I do have more faith in Wise Child's wisdom than I have in my own. She is convinced this is the right thing for us to do, and she has convinced me, or I would not be here. It may take days or weeks or months, but there will be a chance to make things different. Of that I am sure."

I have always liked and trusted Cormac, and I went back to my work feeling more confident about the enterprise.

Meanwhile, I was getting to know some of the other people I worked among. Some of the boys were nice, and we played games together in the evenings, flinging about a rag we made into a ball, swimming in the stream that ran through the castle as the evenings grew warmer, wrestling and teasing one another. I did not like any of the cooks very much—they always seemed to be in a hurry and bad-tempered, perhaps because Meroot demanded so much of them—but I was rather fascinated by a woman who used to come down into the kitchen two or three times a day to give them Meroot's orders. She was thin and elderly, dressed slightly eccentrically in bright-colored silks that did not suit her complexion, but she was cheerful and gave Meroot's orders in a loud, affable voice, ignoring the groans and complaints they often invoked.

"My lady would like stuffed swans for supper with a garnish of blackbirds," she would say. "My lord wishes for a tart of lark's tongue with a dressing of clotted cream and pepper."

I don't know why, but she stuck in my mind as a woman without fear, and this seemed unusual at Caerleon. Even those of us who never saw Meroot and the Gray Knight lived in the knowledge that they were people who inspired dread among their servants. There were stories of horrible punishments inflicted on those who had the misfortune to attend them directly. Even Dame Vawn and the cooks, who rarely met Meroot face-to-face, were afraid of her.

I described the elderly lady, who was called Juliot, to Wise Child, who had never seen her. Then one day, when we were eating our noon meal, Juliot emerged from the kitchens and came out into the sunshine, where she stood for a few moments in the light.

"Quick! Look!" I said to Wise Child. "That's the woman I told you about. That's Dame Juliot."

Wise Child looked at her, and a frown crossed her face. "It's funny," she said. "I feel as if I know her. Only how could I?"

Juliot went back inside the house, and we forgot the conversation for the time being.

It was not till the next day when we were sitting outside in the same place, resting our tired limbs, that suddenly Wise Child gave an exclamation.

"It's the oddest thing," she said. "It cannot be her, but I know who Dame Juliot reminds me of. It's Euny. I met Euny only once, years ago, when she came for the flying—"

"The *flying?*" I interrupted. "You *flew?*"

Wise Child looked momentarily cross. "Well, not *really,*" she said impatiently. "It's hard to explain. But Euny was there, and she seemed . . . oh, donkey's years older than

Dame Juliot. She wore funny black clothes, all ragged, but she was somehow awfully like her."

"Could it be her?" I asked.

"Only if she is able to disguise herself in the most extraordinary way. But then everything Juniper ever told me about Euny did make her sound extraordinary. And if it *is* Euny, she may even know that we are here, and why, and have come out into the yard yesterday 'specially to show us that she is here."

I thought this was a bit far-fetched even for Wise Child, but I agreed that when Juliot appeared again, we must try to talk to her. Since she visited the kitchens daily, the chances were that I would be the one who had the opportunity to speak to her. "What should I say?" I asked.

"You could say that she reminded you of someone, and you wondered if she ever knew a woman called Juniper. If it is not Euny, she will be none the wiser. If it is, we will have made contact." Wise Child's eyes shone at the prospect. For want of anything better to do, I was prepared to try, though I was not as optimistic as she was.

Nearly a week went by before I got my chance. Some days Juliot came and went too quickly for me to speak to her; on other days she was surrounded by people. There was often a certain amount of chaffing and laughter when she was in the kitchen, as if she brought with her some merriment. One day, however, she stood waiting to speak to the head cook as he worked on a sauce too delicate to be interrupted by conversation.

"Dame Juliot," I said, touching her arm to get her attention, "did you ever know someone called Juniper?"

Dame Juliot turned at once and gave me her undivided attention.

"And who wants to know?" she said quite sharply.

"A boy called Colman and a girl called Wise Child," I replied.

"Wise Child?" she said, as if trying the words out. "Those who fly see the world differently." And with that she pushed me out of her way and began to talk to the cook as if he were the only person in the room. It was difficult to wait until noon to speak to Wise Child. There seemed little doubt in my mind that this was indeed Euny.

Wise Child agreed. The very offhandedness of the response reminded her of the Euny she had known and the Euny so often described by Juniper, and even if Juliot habitually behaved in a more friendly fashion, it was as if a touch of the old Euny had showed through.

"I wonder what next," said Wise Child. "She'll surely try and get in touch with us, and then, at last, something will begin to happen!"

CHAPTER EIGHT

Our excitement over the conversation with Juliot was short-lived. On subsequent visits to the kitchens she ignored me, and three weeks went by during which it was hard to keep up our spirits. In my heart I began to believe that we were mistaken. Wise Child, of course, clung to her theory that Juliot was Euny and that my conversation with her had been meaningful.

We toiled away at our work, in my case scrubbing pans, chopping vegetables, cleaning filthy cooking utensils, dragging great pails of water to the cooks, and as often as not getting a clout round the head for my pains. Wise Child's lot was not much better, drawing water from the well, washing clothes, scrubbing floors, and fetching and carrying until every limb ached. By nightfall we were exhausted, especially as we never had quite enough to eat. I was often tempted to say that the whole enterprise was a mistake, but I bit the comment back. I knew that nothing would persuade Wise Child to admit such a thing.

I consoled myself with the thought that even if our

being at Caerleon in such discomfort was pointless, I was there as Wise Child's friend and able to give her companionship and even to make her laugh sometimes. Sometimes, too, one of the nicer cooks would give me a pasty or an apple, which I could share with her, and sometimes, I must admit, I helped myself to food from the kitchen and hid it under my smock. These secret stores were always saved for my times with Wise Child. She, for her part, would get hold of mending thread and a needle with which we repaired my trousers, already nearly worn through from the time I spent on my knees scrubbing, and she managed to find a piece of leather, with which we made a sole for my worn-out shoe. Indeed, the hardships of Caerleon would have been unbearable without the support of each other.

Then, suddenly, everything was different. One day I was plucking a swan in a corner of the big kitchen, a job I disliked since it was difficult to do perfectly and the head cook got very angry if I left any broken feathers behind. I heard the voice of Juliot, louder, more imperious than it usually was, and she swept into the kitchen and pointed a finger at me.

"I want him!" she said.

The head cook shrugged. He knew that Juliot had greater authority than his own.

"What for?" I asked.

"Never mind!" she said brusquely. "You'll find out. Come with me!" She swept up another two boys, then marched into the yard outside and looked around her. By this time Dame Vawn had come to see what was going on, and Juliot soon made it clear what she wanted.

"Line up all the kitchen maids!" she said. "I want some good, strong girls to come and do some work for my lady Meroot. Hurry up! I have not got all day."

In no time about twenty girls were lined up in front of her, but there was no sign of Wise Child.

"Is this all of them?" Juliot asked sharply. Dame Vawn looked along the row.

"One or two may be busy with other work," she said.

"I said I wanted to see *all* the girls, if you remember. My lady told me to pick the strongest." Juliot sat down on the edge of the well, obviously prepared to wait until every single girl had put in an appearance. Dame Vawn, rattled by the mere mention of Meroot's name, hurried off, and soon another half dozen girls, including Wise Child, were herded out into the yard.

"Get in line!" snapped Juliot. "I want to have a good look at you." She went down the line, comparing heights, looking at legs, even feeling the muscles in the girls' arms in a way that I thought quite insulting, almost as a man might inspect a horse before buying it.

"Right!" she said at last, after long and careful comparisons. "I'll take these three." Pushing Wise Child and two other girls before her and snapping her fingers at me and the other boys, she set off up the stairs into the main part of the building that none of us had ever seen. Wise Child and I exchanged glances, and we kept close together.

We climbed flight after flight of stairs, the other boys and girls looking apprehensive as we left behind the dampness and broken woodwork of the lower house and came to a part where there were carpets and tapestries and a glimpse of furnished rooms through doorways. We continued to go higher, and I guessed that Juliot, as a valued servant, lived above the living quarters of her master and mistress. I began to notice how much quieter it was in the castle proper. Without the bustle and noise of the kitchens to disguise it, the sinister feel of Caerleon was abundantly clear.

Finally we came out in a hallway, and Juliot led us along it and into a well-furnished room, where she sat down in a high-backed chair and lined us all up against the opposite wall.

"Let's have a look at you!" she said in a not very friendly tone, very different from the warmth with which I had often heard her joke with the head cook. "Tell me your names!"

Somewhat timidly, not sure what to expect now that they had been taken away from their usual work, the children told their names, and Wise Child and I told ours. Juliot showed no more interest in us than in the others, and I felt doubt that her choosing us had been significant. We had both arrived recently enough to look strong and well fed, while the other children were already showing the signs of poor food and overwork.

"My lady Meroot is giving a party for Prince Brangwyn's birthday," Juliot went on, "and there is much work to be done. The Great Hall and the adjoining rooms must be cleaned and cleaned again. Let me tell you that my lady Meroot will not let you get away with any laziness—the floor must be polished, the tables scrubbed, the glass washed, and the silver shined. One speck of dirt, and someone will suffer for it!"

Juliot said this as if she enjoyed the thought of it.

"The party is in two weeks, and you will work till you drop. You will sleep up here, in the room next door, and if you are lucky you will get a bite to eat sometimes.

"Come then and set to work. There is not too much time if the preparations are to be perfect—as they must be."

She stood up and, leaving us to follow, began to descend the stairs again, until we turned into a stone passage and she hustled us along it. Finally, through several connecting rooms with cupboards and fireplaces and sets of pans and cooking implements hanging from the wall, we emerged first into a small anteroom and then into the Great Hall itself, a vast expanse that seemed far beyond our youthful strength to clean. It was the biggest room I had ever seen. It had a very high ceiling that stretched up into the arching beams. In the center of the hall was a huge fireplace, the smoke of which, when it was alight, went up into a chimney in the ceiling, but not without distributing some soot as it did so. The fireplace itself was black with soot, and we could see soot on the floor and the long wooden tables.

"You," she said to me, "and you and you, carry the tables out one by one and scrub them in the yard outside."

She led us to another room on one side of the hall and gave us scrubbing brushes, brooms and mops, and dusters and pans.

"Get to work!" she said unsympathetically. "I will be back later to see how you get on."

We were all of us scared by Juliot's threats and appalled by the size of the room we had to clean, but although the task seemed quite simply beyond us, everyone set to work, sweeping, washing, and scrubbing. It was Wise Child's misfortune to have to start with the filthy fireplace. With the other boys, I started to drag the tables outside— they were too heavy for us to carry more than a pace or two. They were dirty with old wine and food stains, and we had to scrub them for a long time to make them look any better. It took us the rest of the day to remove the worst of the dirt, and our arms ached with the continous effort. Never well fed in Meroot's household, and therefore perpetually desperate for food, we were given nothing to eat, and by the time Juliot returned we were bitterly hungry.

"You haven't got much done!" was her discouraging remark as she looked around the Great Hall. "You are going to have to work much harder than that!" By this time I had stopped wondering or caring whether she could be Euny. I had decided that whoever she was, I hated her.

Bread and cheese with a few raw onions were then provided for us up in the room where we were going to sleep. I was so tired that I could have settled down for the night there and then, but Juliot chivied us back to our tasks. We had to work another couple of hours before she let us rest.

"Two of you have not been working as hard as the others," she suddenly barked. "Wise Child and Colman, I will see you in my room!" Because I knew that we had worked harder than some of the others and because I had by now given up regarding Juliot in any special light, I was angry as I wearily climbed the stairs once more and slunk into Juliot's private rooms. Wise Child, I knew, felt much the same.

As Wise Child and I entered her room, Juliot had her back to us. She swung round and said to Wise Child, "So! We meet again!" Just for a moment I could see that she was a woman perhaps thirty years older than Juliot, and then once again she was the Juliot with whom I had become familiar.

Both of us gasped at the double transformation.

"I had to disguise myself," she said simply, "or I would never have got the job."

"Euny!" Wise Child exclaimed. "So you are still alive?"

"Of course," said Euny matter-of-factly.

"What are you doing here?"

"I am here, as you are, because I am needed. Great wrongs have been committed by Meroot and the Gray Knight, and it is for the *dorans* to try to restore the balance of goodness. Where is Juniper?"

"In Cornwall, searching for you," I told her.

"She's a good girl," Euny said.

Wise Child and I exchanged an amused glance. It is always funny when grown-ups talk of other grown-ups as if they were mere children, and somehow we had never thought of Juniper, whom we revered, as "a good girl."

Wise Child and I explained how we had all sailed with Finbar to Castle Dore and how Finbar had then gone on to Ireland to buy swords and armor while we came to Caerleon to see if there was any way to help Prince Brangwyn and to defeat Meroot and the Gray Knight.

"The forces are gathering," said Euny softly. "Power within and power without. You need to know what is happening here. Prince Brangwyn is kept a prisoner with all the comforts money can buy. He has an apartment at the top of the castle with everything he needs to amuse him, except that he is barely allowed out of the castle grounds, and he was a boy who loved his hunting and hawking. They feed him on stories of his return to Castle Dore. When the time is ripe, they tell him, and they encourage him to believe that that will be after his eighteenth birthday. I know this only because I have overheard conversations. What I don't know is whether he believes them or whether he is going along with them and watching his chance. Once or twice I have heard him raging angrily at them, but I have never been able to hear what the conversation is about."

"So they haven't used magic on him?" Wise Child asked.

"No," Euny said. "I think their plan must be to make Prince Brangwyn so comfortable that he will become idle and indifferent. I don't know for sure, but somehow I doubt that can work. He is not his father's son for nothing, nor his mother's neither, and at eighteen there is courage and energy in plenty. But he must feel very alone."

She paused. "That is where we come in. You need to know that Meroot is seriously ill. Not mortally ill as yet, though it may come to that. She is often in pain, and that is where I am useful to her. She has discovered that by touching her with oils I can ease her pain, and so I have become indispensable. That apart, as you have noticed, I am a sort of lady of the chamber, who runs various errands for her, which means that I can be close to her and, indeed, almost anywhere else in the castle without arousing suspicion. She trusts me because she needs to. Still, it is not easy. She is a woman of violent temper, which terrifies most people who work for her. My strength is that I am not afraid of her."

"So what next?" asked Wise Child.

"I need accomplices," Euny said, "if only to keep watch if I try to get to Prince Brangwyn. That, by the way, is a dangerous undertaking, since if by any chance he has sided with Meroot and the knight, he could give me away. So it needs careful thought."

"But surely . . . ," said Wise Child, shocked. "Prince Brangwyn . . . I mean, he wouldn't . . ."

"He wouldn't under normal circumstances, but shut up as he is, cut off from anyone who cares about Castle Dore, yes, he might do or think anything, even come to see things from his captors' point of view. And little blame to him. It can happen to the best people, and Brangwyn is little more than a boy. Somehow, though, I feel that part of things will be all right."

I was surprised to hear Euny speak of the prince by his Christian name, without title. But Wise Child had told me that Euny had always enjoyed a special intimacy with Juniper's family.

Euny went on. "I recognized Wise Child as soon as I saw her, of course, and then when Colman spoke to me that day, I knew what I had to do, and who my helpers would be."

"Did you come here without a plan, then?" Wise Child asked, fascinated.

"Of course. As I suspect you did. In difficult circumstances like these, as you guessed, you have to work your way gradually into the problem, like a puzzle you have to solve. It's no good making up your mind in advance to something that may be quite impossible when you are on the spot. All I knew before I came was that I must disguise myself, and then try to make myself invaluable to Meroot. So! When the cleaning of the Great Hall is finished, I shall send the other boys and girls back to their duties and try to keep you two with me as my assistants. The big feast Meroot and the knight are giving for Brangwyn's birthday is probably going to be the chance we need. But I must emphasize that this is all very risky. Meroot is full of a twisted kind of magic, but she is not without insight. If she was not so ill, she might guess what I was up to. If you help me, you, too, will be exposed to danger. Are you ready for that?"

"Indeed we are," said Wise Child with enthusiasm. "I came here longing to help the prince and to confound Meroot and the Gray Knight, and though Juniper thought I was too young, the dreaming bundle confirmed that I was right to do so."

"How did you get hold of the dreaming bundle?" Euny suddenly asked in her sharp way, and for a moment I once again caught sight of the very old and wrinkled woman who was concealed within the body of Juliot.

Wise Child explained about my and Cormac's visit to the Mother's hut and the protections she had bestowed upon us.

"The tools for the task," Euny said dreamily. "I trust you have brought the remaining tools with you."

"We have," said Wise Child. "Though I live in terror of them being found. I carry them about with me most of the time."

151

Euny suddenly appeared to change the subject.

"I have never forgotten the night of your flying," she said. "Never have I seen another child take to it like you did, like a duck to water."

"But surely Juniper . . ." Wise Child was obviously uncomfortable that a comparison might be made.

"She was older than you, and her flying was a more low-key affair. It differs from one *doran* to another."

"I don't remember you paying me any compliments at the time. In fact, I thought you were rather rude," Wise Child said robustly.

Euny chuckled. "My bark was always worse than my bite," she said. "And if I had been too kind to you, the flying would never have happened. Juniper was inclined to be soft with you."

"She was kind," said Wise Child, disagreeing.

"Kindness is not always the best method. Not when something hard has to be done." A silence fell among us, which was as eloquent as if Wise Child had argued. She would never brook any criticism of Juniper.

Something was bothering me.

"Where does Cormac fit into all this?" I asked.

"Not sure!" said Euny airily. "He will have his place, have no fear. Time for you to go to bed," she continued in her most dictatorial tones. "Obviously, you will keep this conversation to yourselves—easy for you, since you speak little Cornish. Pretend to be upset that I have scolded you and carry on as you did today. Nothing much will happen for a bit. If you see me wearing a red headdress, you will know that I need to speak to you, one or both of you. One might be less obvious. Come to my room—around noon—and I will usually be here."

It was like Euny, I was to discover, not to say that she was sorry the work was hard or to try to reassure us in any way at all. Wise Child explained to me that Euny had little concept of hardship. Her own childhood had been bitterly hard, and she had learned to be careless of hardship for herself or for others.

In spite of this, however, I found myself now beginning to like and trust her. Wise Child felt the same. If anything was to have an effect at Caerleon, it would need someone as strong as Euny to set it up. We decided we were content to do as she told us. If we were somewhat frightened at what we were taking on—and we were—at least it gave us something to think about during our tedious working days.

In the time we had been at Caerleon, we had never seen either Meroot or the Gray Knight. Not surprising, really, since we were confined to the kitchen area. Stories had filtered into the kitchen of Meroot ordering beatings and worse punishments for those who had annoyed her, and once or twice, as we worked in the Great Hall, I had heard a harsh female voice in the distance raised in anger, castigating some unfortunate servant, and had guessed that it must be her. The ugly note in her voice was chilling.

But then the day came when Meroot entered the Great Hall to see for herself how the preparations were going. As bad luck would have it, we were having our brief midday rest. She entered silently, perhaps hoping to catch us in just such an idle moment, and when she saw that she had succeeded, she smiled a cruel smile. It was hard to believe that she was related to Juniper. She had sandy-colored hair strongly marked with gray, and cold, pale blue eyes that swept swiftly over the room and the exhausted workers. She was very thin and her face was haggard, obviously marked by her illness. She wore a yellow silk dress, in itself beautiful and lavishly cut, but the color did little for her sallow complexion and wasted body. A short way behind her came Euny.

"So this is how you work!" she said scornfully.

"It is disgraceful, my lady!" Euny said. "I shall see that they work extra-long hours tonight before they get any supper."

"Supper!" said Meroot. "There will be no supper for them!"

"Very well, my lady," said Euny, with a respectful lowering of her head. "Such laziness must not be encouraged."

In fact, the Great Hall was looking a great deal cleaner after all our efforts. The soot was gone, and the floors and most of the tables shone. We were now in the final stages of our preparations. Plates and glasses had been washed till they sparkled, and the silver glowed in the mid-day light.

"We should be finished in here tomorrow, my lady," Euny said in the dulcet tones she used for Meroot. "The workers can then return to their usual duties—they will be needed in the kitchens, of course. If you agree, I would like to keep a couple of them by me to run errands for you and generally help with the birthday arrangements."

"Mmm," said Meroot. "Why not? This table has a smear on it and must be polished again. Indeed, I want all the tables polished again!"

"Very well, my lady."

Listlessly we set to work, and Meroot stood and watched, urging us to put more energy into the task.

"Perhaps we need to find ways of making you work harder," she said nastily. "It's amazing how a beating can increase a servant's enthusiasm."

I have never forgotten the frightened faces of our fellow workers as they tried desperately to force their tired arms to rub harder. We were all very relieved when Meroot left the room.

Euny followed Meroot's instructions about seeing that we got no supper, and since we had had no lunch and had worked hard all day, we went very miserably to bed.

"She's got to appear to be Meroot's obedient servant," said Wise Child to me, determined to be loyal. I saw her point, of course, but I felt the anger of being badly treated.

Next morning, however, I noticed that our breakfast was quite a bit more substantial than usual. That morning, also, Euny was wearing a red headdress. On the pretense of getting some more of the wax we used for polishing, Wise Child made her way to Euny's room as soon as we had finished eating. I could tell by the gleam in her eye when she came out that events had moved on in some way. Thanks to the convenience of being able to talk in our own language, she could tell me the news right away, though she did her best to talk in a rather dull tone of voice, in contrast to the amazing thing she was about to tell me.

"We are going to see the prince!" she said. "Meroot has asked Euny to discuss his birthday arrangements with him. She is not sure why Meroot has suggested this, though it may be because she thinks it will come better from someone else. She is to talk the plans through with him, and she is taking us with her because we are her assistants. Isn't that amazing?"

"When?"

"Tomorrow. We shall finish work in the Great Hall today, and then even Euny thinks we should clean ourselves up a bit. She is going to try to find some decent clothes for us, and I can wash my hair tonight."

The whole thing did seem a kind of miracle, that we should get close to the heart of what ailed Castle Dore. Perhaps too much of a miracle.

"Do you think it's a trap?" I had to ask. "Maybe

Meroot suspects Euny and is giving her this chance to betray herself?"

"Euny thinks not, and you know, she is pretty shrewd. But as she said before, there is enormous risk here. No one—not her and maybe not Meroot—is sure where Prince Brangwyn's loyalties lie. Euny will have to tread very carefully, but even then, it may not save her . . . and us. She thinks, and I think, too, that it is a risk that we have to run if we are to have any chance of saving the situation."

As usual, I seemed to be the one most burdened with fears and doubts. It occurred to me, really for the first time, that it was not so much my own skin that I feared risking (though I would prefer not to die) but Wise Child's. I did not like the thought of her in danger, but since she seemed determined to get into dangerous situations, I had no choice but to accompany her.

"Well, that's good," I said without much enthusiasm. Wise Child looked at me and laughed.

"It'll be all right," she said. "I feel it in my bones."

I am not sure that even Wise Child's bones were quite so confident the next day when we climbed the stairs to Prince Brangwyn's tower apartment, trying hard to keep up with Euny's brisk pace. Wise Child wore a quite respectable red dress, and her long, dark hair rippled over her shoulders. I noticed that she had become thinner during our time at Caerleon, but also taller and prettier. I, too, was wearing more becoming clothes—a pair of trousers without holes or patches that more or less fitted me and a shirt and jacket.

"What are *we* here for?" Wise Child asked Euny. "What will he think we could do that you could not?"

"Let us hope that does not occur to him," Euny said. "My hope is that he might feel more like talking to people nearer to his age than I am. Children may seem safer to him. If you see the chance to get into conversation with him, do so."

I thought of our broken Cornish. Although we both spoke it much better than when we first arrived, Wise Child in particular, we still had a long way to go.

The furnishings became grander as we ascended the stairs to Prince Brangwyn's apartment in the tower. There were flags and banners, at least one of which was the flag of King Mark, I noted, as well as suits of armor and spears, until the stairs became too narrow. We arrived at a room also decorated with armor and some heads of wild boars, which reminded me that the Gray Knight was a passionate hunter. At the end of this room was an elegant door on which Euny knocked boldly. A footman opened the door, and we were ushered through a hallway and into one of the most splendid rooms I had ever seen.

I used to think Juniper had the most amazing rooms when I first visited her at the white house on the island, but Prince Brangwyn's rooms were even more wonderful. Against walls of dark wood there were tapestries of a luminous green illustrating hunting scenes, some of them so lifelike that I felt as if one of the stags might at any moment leap into the room. The magnificent carpet depicted Castle Dore in its great days (I suspected it had been stolen from the castle when it was sacked). On a shelf were some books and a beautifully carved piece of ivory. At a round table inlaid with precious stones sat the young prince in a finely carved chair, a chessboard in front of him. Beside it lay a slate, on which we could see a few words had been scribbled. He rose at our entrance.

Unlike Meroot, Prince Brangwyn bore a distinct, indeed an uncanny, resemblance to Juniper. He had her black hair, which he wore very short and curly, soldier-fashion, and her deep brown eyes, but it was the expression on his face, an air of natural wisdom, that reminded me most of her, even though in his case there was also something sulky and discontented in his look, the lips not far from a pout.

Euny and Wise Child curtsied and I bowed, and then Brangwyn said, "Please sit."

Brangwyn sank languidly into his chair, as if he had no energy, no interest in anything, even the sight of strangers.

Euny introduced herself and Wise Child and me and then said, "We have come here at the request of my lady Meroot to discuss the plans for your birthday, to tell you what she has already planned, and to ask you if there are other diversions you would like."

"And what has she planned?" The tone was petulant.

"As you know, you are to be crowned *regulus* of Cornwall on your birthday, and then there will be a feast in the Great Hall for a hundred knights and their ladies. The cooks will prepare wild boar and venison and other meats for this, and it is assumed that it will go on for several days. The Gray Knight has reserved some of his finest wines for the occasion."

Prince Brangwyn did not look particularly excited at the thought, and I could imagine why. Much as I might have enjoyed eating venison and wild boar, I would have had no taste myself for spending days doing nothing but eating and drinking, even though the time would doubtless be enlivened with music and stories.

"So who is to be invited to this dinner?"

"The kings and princes from neighboring countries," Euny said. "From Wales, England, even from Ireland, I believe. You are to be formally presented as *regulus* of Cornwall."

Prince Brangwyn raised a skeptical eyebrow. "I do not rule anyone or anything," he said shortly.

Euny seemed to think it best to ignore this.

"There are other plans afoot," she went on. "A racing of horses, a visit of players and storytellers, wrestling, maybe some jousting."

"Perhaps you could ask Meroot if I shall take part in the racing or the jousting," the prince said.

"I think she would fear for your highness's safety," said Euny.

"But I am the best horseman for miles around, as she knows very well. And no mean fighter, either."

"It does not surprise me," Euny said, "knowing your ancestry."

"I would like to visit Castle Dore in memory of my parents and to talk to the people among whom I grew up," the prince continued. "I would like Erc, the famous harpist of Castle Dore, to come and play at my birthday feast."

Behind Brangwyn's words, which were vehemently said, I could sense other longings, the longing to be free to go where he wanted in the world, not to be imprisoned in his young manhood in the dreariness of Caerleon, where he had no young companions.

Euny bowed slightly, as if she had taken in his wishes, and continued, "I will pass on your wishes to my lady."

"Who will veto them."

Euny might have said more, but Wise Child irrepressibly said, "Do you play the harp yourself, your highness? I do. Though I have not played lately, and one's fingers soon get unfitted for it."

The prince seemed to come out of a dark reverie and looked at her as if he had only just seen her. He had a lovely smile.

"Where do you come from?" he asked. "I can tell you are not a Cornish girl."

"I come from Dalriada in the far north," said Wise Child hesitatingly, wondering how to explain the length of her journey.

"Dalriada," echoed the prince with a strange expression on his face, and for a moment I wondered if he would say more.

"Her father is a sailor and a trader, and she sometimes accompanies him on voyages," said Euny smoothly. "He is trading in Ireland, and meanwhile, Wise Child is working at Caerleon."

"And learning to speak Cornish. . . . Yes, I do play the harp," he went on. "Sometime you must play for me, and I will play for you."

"I was wondering," said Wise Child boldly, looking at the chessboard, "if you had decided what the next move was going to be."

The prince shook his head.

"May I?" she asked, and without waiting for his response, she moved one of the knights. Slowly, thoughtfully, the two of them began to play. Euny and I smiled at each other. If Wise Child and the prince could form a sort of friendship by means of chess and the harp, so much the better.

While Euny and I sat and watched, the game continued. The prince seemed more animated, cheerful, in a way that was not apparent when we first arrived, and his good spirits survived even Wise Child's checkmate.

"You are a good player," he said. "I am not a very good player, but it passes the time. I also write poetry." He indicated the slate beside him with the few words scrawled upon it. "You don't know a rhyme for 'winter,' do you?"

We shook our heads, and there was a silence, and then he hesitantly said, "Do any of you happen to know a place called Castle Dore?"

CHAPTER NINE

In our moments of leisure, usually late in the evening, Wise Child and I often talked of Finbar and Juniper and wondered how they were getting on. I described to Wise Child the way Juniper had brightened when she decided to make the journey to Euny's country, and how I thought it was a way of throwing off her grief and fear about the risk Wise Child was running.

It was much later, of course, before we heard the story of Juniper's pilgrimage from her own lips, but I am telling it here because this was what was going on while Wise Child and I were trying to establish a friendship with Prince Brangwyn. Juniper had retraced the steps of her original autumn journey on the day she left Castle Dore as a young girl and went to be Euny's pupil, and the path along the river and through the wood brought back powerful memories of that important day. This time, unlike that first time, she had provided herself sensibly with food and water, although now it was a day in spring, not hot, but pleasant with some warm sunshine.

I wonder quite what she expected to find, and even when I questioned her closely, she could not really tell me. She simply knew that it was a visit she had to make and that it was one, she hoped, that would give her the clues she needed about Euny's whereabouts. Although she had heard nothing of her for so long, in her heart she was sure that Euny was alive.

Juniper had a deep love and respect for Euny, though she had been a harsh mistress to her. Oddly, perhaps because she had enjoyed such a privileged and comfortable life at home, it had changed her in ways she was later grateful for, though it was all terribly painful at the time. It had set her free, as she once said to me, and made her certain that a *doran* was what she must be. And, of course, she became a very good one, healing many people and giving comfort and courage to many more.

She arrived in the late afternoon at Euny's hut, which she found in the condition that Cormac and I had described, ripped and slashed apart with violent ax strokes. Since she had once lived there for a year with Euny, it must have been infinitely more disturbing to her to see it destroyed than it had been for Cormac and me. Even we, for whom the place had no associations, had both been shocked and upset by the sight.

Juniper told me that she had stood by the ruin for some time, talking out loud to Euny as if she were there, asking her for some sign and also for help in the task of saving Castle Dore. She said that she kept getting the oddest feeling that Euny was still there and looking kindly upon her, but whether because she was dead and looking down from heaven at one of her favorite pupils, or elsewhere on earth, Juniper was not sure. She *did* know that Euny could appear and disappear when she chose to, and she rather hoped that she might suddenly materialize on this occasion, but nothing else happened . . . then.

Juniper took it into her head that rather than climb to the Mother's hut and seek shelter for the night as Cormac and I had done, she would leave that till the morrow. For the moment she wanted to commune with the spirit of Euny in the place where she had lived for so long. She felt she could not tear herself away from it. There was nowhere dry enough to sleep, and although the day had been warm, the night would certainly be cold. She decided that in devotion to her teacher, she would bear that, and she went and sat down on the coarse bricks at the edge of the well, where on so many occasions she had been sent to draw water. She felt oddly peaceful, really for the first time since she had parted with Wise Child.

She was not quite sure afterward whether she fell asleep or simply moved into a sort of trance, but then she heard a harsh chuckle and Euny's inimitable voice saying, "Didn't want to let her go, did you? But she was too much for you."

At that she woke up, or came out of the trance, and

looked wildly round, thinking to see Euny, but there was no sign of her.

"Euny! Euny!" she begged out loud. "Please come and help me. I have let my beloved Wise Child go, and I do not know what will become of her. I cannot bear the destruction of Castle Dore, nor the way the knight and Meroot have degraded the people. I don't know what to do. It is too difficult for me. And I need to see you, not just hear your voice."

And then from behind her she heard Euny.

"You always did want your own way!"

Juniper spun round, and Euny was standing behind her. With tears running down her cheeks, Juniper embraced her.

"That will do!" said Euny, who was never a great one for endearments.

"I thought you might be dead," said Juniper.

"Certainly not! What call have I to die? There are many important things to be seen to first, Castle Dore among others."

"But where have you been?"

"Here and there," said Euny vaguely. "Mostly there. At the moment I am at Caerleon."

"At Caerleon! What are you doing there?"

"I felt my help was needed. Let me tell you, I have a very grand job at the castle. I am more or less Meroot's boon companion. She is very sick and often in pain, and I have used the healing arts—some of which I picked up from you, by the way, since healing was never my forte—in gaining her confidence. So I have the run of the place. In disguise. You wouldn't know me; I look so young when I am there, and I wear the fanciest clothes."

Just then Euny was wearing the torn, drab clothes in which Juniper had always seen her and looked extremely old, her face covered in wrinkles, her hands thin and clawlike.

"I can scarcely believe it," said Juniper.

"Have I ever told you a lie?"

"Never. It is just that . . . you are always such a surprise. But Wise Child? How is she?"

"Striking up a friendship with Prince Brangwyn. They play chess together and entertain each other on the harp. Lucky you taught her those fancy things. She'd never have learned them from *me*!" Euny sniffed contemptuously.

"So she is safe?"

"For the time being. Though it might change at any moment. Caerleon Castle is a cruel, dangerous place in which to be. She's a good girl, though, that Wise Child. She knows how to survive, I think, and Colman, too. He is a good, loyal friend who won't let any harm come to her, if he can help it."

"And Cormac?"

"They made him a sort of under-footman. He is not beautiful enough to be seen in company, which puts him in a fairly safe position. But he does not see much of the children, and I am not sure how he fits into the puzzle, though I suppose he does."

"The puzzle?"

"The puzzle of how to help the people of Castle Dore, and, of course, Prince Brangwyn. They have all suffered quite enough."

"The prince? Tell me about him."

"He looks uncannily like you. We are all agreed about that. It is risky for us to say too much. We are not quite sure of his relationship with Meroot, whether somehow she has got him in her power. But he seems angry, frustrated, and homesick for Castle Dore and tired of being shut up where he can do nothing."

"Surely that is all you need to know?"

"Maybe. But maybe it is a trick, and he will betray us to Meroot. He has been in her power for a long time and that can change people. Also, freedom, though he thinks he wants it, may frighten him too much."

Juniper looked doubtful.

"My father's son . . . ," she began.

"I know, I know. But I have seen the situation, and you have not, or not recently. The cruelty and venom of Meroot know no bounds, more so since she begins to think her sickness may be deadly. The knight, I think, loves her, would do anything for her, including carrying out her most wicked schemes, like the plunder and starvation of the people of Castle Dore. So we wait and see how it goes with the prince."

"But what can I do to help?" Juniper asked desperately.

"First of all, return to Castle Dore. Finbar will be back before long, and the people will need you there to give them the courage to take and use the weapons. Then you must make your way to the castle for Prince Brangwyn's eighteenth birthday celebration."

"What? Meroot would recognize me instantly!"

"Disguise yourself!"

"I am not sure I can."

"Of course, you do have a way of being thoroughly yourself all the time. I've never met anyone who was so bad at pretending anything. But I think you will have to do it. There will be many, many people there, so you will not stand out from the crowd unless you choose to do so."

"Oh, Euny, it sounds awfully difficult!"

"I did not say that it was easy, but we can do most things if we try, and there is much at stake here."

"But I'm sorry, I don't see the point. Of course I will go to Caerleon if you think that is what I must do, but what use am I going to be?"

"It will concentrate the power," said Euny solemnly. "You, me, Wise Child—that is three *dorans,* more than equal to the trumpery magic of Meroot and the Gray Knight. And that little boy, Colman. He's got the *doran*'s power, it seems to me. Or at least a touch of it."

"But he doesn't want to become a *doran,*" Juniper said. "He told me he wants to be ordinary."

"God bless the boy," Euny said. "That *is* his power. Not craving it. All the same, he is a good chap to have around."

Juniper smiled at Euny's untypical use of a word. Euny lived in the past in some ways, and Juniper had never before heard her use a word like "chap."

Euny shook herself then, a bit like a dog that has been swimming.

"I think that is all I have to say at present, and I had better get back to Caerleon because even I cannot be in two places at once. Annoyingly. Some people can, you know. I must be back by suppertime or there will be trouble."

"Please don't go!" Juniper told us that she sounded like a child herself when she said this, but Euny, always the most willful of people, turned and was gone. Totally gone. There was not a trace of her in the whole clearing.

Juniper felt even more stupefied by Euny's disappearance than she had been by her sudden appearance, but after a little, she thought there was nothing more useful to do than to set off back home. She had found out what she had come to seek, and although she was tired, it was too cold and she was too excited by what she had heard to sleep in any case. She turned and walked back the way she had come. The only immediate comfort she could think of was that Wise Child appeared to be safe, at least for the time being, and that she would soon see Finbar.

❂ ❂ ❂

Meanwhile, Wise Child and I were getting to know Prince Brangwyn. I felt that he preferred Wise Child to me. Her Cornish was better, and she could amuse him by playing chess with him and playing the harp for him. But he was courteous to me, asking whether I missed my own country and what things I liked to do. I realized that he thought I was Wise Child's brother, and it was easy to let him believe it. What neither of us dared to do was to lead the conversation to a place where we would get to know his true feelings, and in any case, Euny had forbidden it. We knew that he was often sad, bored, and angry, but whether he accepted it as inevitable (he had spent months at Caerleon already, after all, after seeing his home destroyed) or dreamed of escape or revolution, it was impossible to know. His training as a prince had taught him to hide his feelings and to be cautious with his tongue.

"What do you think he feels?" I asked Wise Child once.

"I wish I knew. I like him, but I hate the feeling that one wrong word from us might get us betrayed to Meroot."

Oddly, it was later that day that we met Meroot in his room. He sent for us most afternoons. Euny used to go to see him in the mornings to take his instructions, or so she said, though he seemed to have very little interest in the forthcoming feast, and it was through her that we got his orders. Judging by Meroot's surprise at seeing us, I do not think she knew of our acquaintance with the prince. Fortunately, we were just sitting and talking when she arrived—

not playing chess or doing anything else that suggested we knew each other quite well.

"These two are taking my orders for my birthday celebrations," he said, introducing us formally.

"They seem very young," said Meroot. She eyed us suspiciously. I wondered whether she would remember seeing us before in the crowd of children in the Great Hall, but, of course, she had never really considered those children as individuals or looked at them properly, and in any case, we were quite differently dressed.

Meroot did look ill. She was pale and gaunt, with a yellow tinge to her face, and her eyes were almost feverishly bright. Still, I had the disconcerting sense that she was looking right through me. Then she winced, as if a severe pain was passing through her. If she had been anyone else, I would have felt pity, but Meroot was so pitiless herself that I armed myself against sympathy.

"We have struck up something of a friendship," the prince went on. "They amuse me, and Wise Child here plays the harp rather beautifully."

"Mmm," said Meroot dourly. "I am glad to hear it." It struck me that it was in her interest to keep the prince happy—he was less trouble that way. But the prince's need to explain us to Meroot revealed that he recognized her power over him and was obedient to it. Or was he merely pretending and watching his chance for escape?

When she had gone, the prince shrugged a little.

"Mustn't fall out with Auntie Meroot!" he remarked, but in a rueful voice, as if his acquiescence gave him shame.

I certainly felt pity for him. Very nearly eighteen years old, strong, handsome, intelligent, trained to be a king but kept at Castle Caerleon like an animal in a cage with no real life of his own. How long could Meroot keep him there, and what could she be planning to do with him?

We discussed this point with Euny, who demanded to know every detail of our meeting.

"At some point," Wise Child remarked, "we are going to have to take the risk of making Prince Brangwyn reveal his real feelings."

"Not yet!" said Euny.

"Then when?"

"We'll know. Do it too soon, and it will ruin everything. I forbid you to speak to him in that way."

Wise Child nodded, but I was not sure that she agreed.

Meanwhile, the preparations for the prince's birthday continued. Meroot had refused to let the prince visit Castle Dore, though she agreed that Erc, the blind harpist, should be allowed to come and play for him at the feast. The horse race was planned on the day before his birthday. The prince took us to see his horse, a magnificent bay animal called Golden, who had his own stable at the foot of the prince's tower. It had come with him from Castle Dore. Indeed, he had been tied to its back to make the journey to Caerleon.

Now he was allowed to ride him once a day but always accompanied by soldiers, who would prevent him from riding too far from the castle.

"I would really like to take part in the horse race," the prince said sadly. "Meroot pretends that it is the risk of injury that is the problem. In fact, her fear is that I will ride away, escape." As he spoke, he looked over the fields into the distance, as if he longed to go there. But then he added despondently, "But where is there to go?"

There was a long silence between us, and then Wise Child, coming near to breaking her promise to Euny, said, "Would you like to escape?"

The prince didn't respond, but I thought I saw tears in his eyes. It was at that moment that I knew I felt love for this new friend, that I longed to help him into a happier future. Certainly a happy future did not lie here for him, pampered like a lap dog by Meroot.

As always now, Wise Child and I discussed the meeting afterward.

"You came close to breaking your agreement with Euny," I said, still slightly shocked at the recollection.

"But don't you see, we got some information from him. We have opportunities that Euny does not have, to get close to him, to make him feel that he can trust us."

"Euny would say, 'Can we trust him?' If he betrayed us to Meroot, she would probably have us killed, and then where would he be?"

"It is dangerous. I know that," said Wise Child uneasily. "It's just that . . . well, I cannot quite see what Euny has in mind. And I am not sure she sees a way forward herself."

"Euny does not work like that, thinking it all out cleverly beforehand. She takes each day as it comes and goes entirely by what she feels on any particular day."

"That has its uses, I see that, and I see also that she is a very great *doran*. But I am a *doran*, too, or someone on the way to being one, and I have my own knowledge. I know it sounds conceited, but I have, and it makes a difference."

"I believe you," I said.

When we saw Prince Brangwyn the next day, he seemed more reserved with us, as if he felt he had revealed too much the day before, and we kept the conversation light. It was a bright, sunny day, and we went out to the butts, where he had already begun to teach us archery, something that had been part of his careful education. I was delighted to find that I was much cleverer at it than Wise Child, who became crosser and crosser as I hit the target at greater and greater distances.

"Colman is better at letting the arrow go than you are," the prince told her. "You want to control it. That is not quite how it works."

Wise Child frowned. "Of course I want to control it."

The prince laughed. "Well, try to be more lighthearted about it. The secret is in the letting go."

We went back to his room, where Wise Child sang rather beautifully to the harp, which cheered her up somewhat. She always needed to succeed.

When she had finished, the prince stretched and yawned. "Meroot is coming soon. I guess you'd better go. You know, I am so grateful to you both. You make life better for me."

Then Wise Child did something that surprised me. She bent and kissed him gently on the cheek.

"We love coming," she said lightly. I thought he might feel that the kiss was an offense to his princely dignity, but he seemed pleased and smiled up at her. "Come tomorrow!" he said.

"Phew!" I said on the stairs. "That was a bit daring!"

"I know," Wise Child said. "It just came over me. I didn't think about it. You know, I am beginning to love the prince. Really."

"Me too!" I said.

Just then we saw Meroot coming along the passage toward us. She was a long way off and had her head down. Wise Child grabbed me by the sleeve and pulled me into a side room. We held our breath as Meroot paused by the door, her head up as if listening for something, then continued on.

"Better she does not know that we see the prince quite so often," said Wise Child as we made our way back to Euny, and I agreed with her. In any case, I was always glad of any chance to avoid Meroot and her pale, chilling glance.

On our next visit to the prince, he seemed in a bad mood. He replied to our comments shortly, and his head was sunk on his hand, something I had noticed occurred on his darker days.

"Something's wrong," said Wise Child daringly.

He hesitated and then said, "Yes, there is." He had hoped that somehow he could persuade Meroot to let him ride in the birthday horse race, but she had forbidden it. He didn't go on to say this, but it obviously made the feeling of being a leashed bird particularly galling.

"I *want* Golden to be in the race," he said, petulant as a child. Then, as if the thought had just struck him, he turned to me and said, "You could not ride him for me, I suppose."

I shook my head. Except in Ireland, I had barely ridden a horse at all, and even if I had, I was too small for a horse with the size and strength of Golden.

"I know!" said Wise Child, physically starting as the idea struck her. "Cormac! He's a wonderful horseman!"

"Cormac?" echoed the prince. "Who is he?"

"He's an under-footman here, and a friend of ours. Really, he is wonderful with horses."

The prince nodded.

"What's to lose?" he said. He got up and left the room for a moment. He had a servant who sat permanently outside his apartment to run messages for him.

"Winnol!" we heard him say. "I want you to find an under-footman called Cormac and bring him to me at once." It struck me that Meroot allowed him this sort of liberty with her staff as a way of making him feel that he was still a little in charge of his life.

When Cormac arrived, I could see that his scarred and ugly appearance was something of a shock to the prince.

"This is our very dear friend Cormac," Wise Child said emphatically. "Cormac, the prince is looking for a man to ride his horse, Golden, at the birthday race. We have been recommending you as the best horseman we know."

Cormac at once looked alarmed, as well he might. "I don't know about that," he said.

"There is only one way to find out," the prince said firmly. "We will meet at the stables after the noontide meal. If anyone questions your leaving your work, say that it is on Prince Brangwyn's orders."

"Yes, your highness," said Cormac.

It was a lovely, warm afternoon as the prince saddled Golden and led him out to the field. I was aware that he was carefully watched by two of the soldiers, one of whom started putting a saddle on a horse rather quickly, as if to follow him. Noticing this, the prince brusquely said, "I am not riding today."

The prince gave Cormac a leg-up onto Golden, and Cormac gently walked and trotted him in a circle, as if to show the prince that he knew how to handle a horse. Almost from the beginning, rider and horse seemed at ease together, as if Golden knew and appreciated a good master when he felt him on his back, and as if Cormac knew a magnificent horse when it moved beneath him. He came trotting back and bowed a little to the prince as he reached us, his enthusiasm driving away his shyness.

"He's lovely!" he said. "It's a privilege to ride such an animal!"

The prince glowed at this admiration of his darling.

Cormac set off again, cantering this time, then slowly and gracefully moving into a gallop. Golden's speed was an amazing sight. Cormac galloped back, slowing well before he reached the prince.

"Very good!" said the prince. "You move well together. Now I want you to make him go flat out."

Cormac set off once again, and if I had been amazed by Golden's earlier turn of speed, this time I was even more astonished. I could hear Wise Child beside me, as excited as I was, cheering him on, and I could see the smile on the prince's face. All he said was, "He'll do!" but from the warmth with which he greeted Cormac when he returned with the sweating Golden, I knew that he was delighted.

"I want you to ride for me in the birthday race," said the prince. "You will wear my colors of purple and yellow— I will have the suit specially made for you—and let me tell you that I expect you to win!"

"I'll do my best, sir."

Cormac was sent back to his duties, though not before we had managed to exchange a little information about how life was going for him—not very happily—in the castle. Wise Child and I made our way back to Euny's apartment, feeling a bit flat after the excitement of the afternoon.

CHAPTER TEN

"What's wrong with Cormac's face?" the prince asked us curiously the next day.

"He had leprosy," Wise Child replied, "and then a healer cured him, though she couldn't get rid of the scars."

"My sister was—is, I suppose—a healer. In Dalriada. Where you come from. I have not seen her for many years. My parents could not understand how someone with her background and education could want to go off and live among peasants, and I was really too young to think about it, but it was odd."

"She must have been a rather special sort of person," said Wise Child.

"Yes, I think she was. I wondered if you ever heard tell of her. Her name was Ninnoc, though I believe the local people had their own name for her."

"It is a large country, Dalriada," Wise Child said, without having to lie.

Sitting there, looking into eyes so like Juniper's while the prince talked of her, was a strange experience.

The prince and Cormac began to meet regularly in the afternoon to exercise Golden and for Cormac to practice racing him. Quite often we went along, too, and while Prince Brangwyn rode on his horse, we got the chance to talk at length to Cormac. We told him all about our sessions with Euny, our friendship with the prince, and the encouraging sense that somehow some plan was coming together, though we did not quite know how. (At this stage, Euny had said nothing to us about meeting Juniper. It was like her to withhold information.)

Cormac was relieved to be in touch with us again. He had felt a certain responsibility for Wise Child when they had set off together and had felt bad that he barely saw her when they both started work at Caerleon. My arrival there had made him feel better. Euny's presence was also deeply comforting to him, as, of course, it was to us.

"It is impossible to understand how it can all work out," he said. "One just has to trust in the power of the *dorans*. But it is difficult to see how Caerleon, with all its power, could ever be overthrown."

He shared the fear of Meroot that was common to all the workers in the castle. They would do almost anything to avoid coming face-to-face with her. But most of his working hours had been spent performing humble tasks in the Gray Knight's apartment.

"What is he like?" Wise Child asked.

"Handsome. As cruel as Meroot and much cleverer

than her. If anyone will catch Euny out in her plans, it will be him."

Much of the time, talking to the prince and listening to Euny, we could pretend to ourselves that what we were engaged upon—trying to find a way to save and restore Castle Dore—was not as dangerous as all that. But comments such as Cormac's would remind us again that we could easily lose our lives, probably in a terribly painful way. Even Wise Child turned paler as he talked.

I noticed that when Wise Child talked to Euny, she pushed her to let her take greater risks in conversation with the prince, to let him realize, at least partially, that we were his allies. Privately Wise Child said to me, "I don't think she understands how close we are to the prince."

Cautious as ever, I had a lot of sympathy with Euny. Wise Child's boldness was all very good, but one sentence too far would be irretrievable. It would expose the prince's attitude to Meroot, whether of rebellion or subservience, and that in turn would expose us. Yet the birthday celebration was coming closer, and we were pretty sure that Euny's intention was for something dramatic to occur then.

Euny had a way of snubbing Wise Child whenever she tried to bring the subject up, which I thought was a great mistake. Wise Child could respond to reason, but she had too firm a belief in her own powers to let Euny put her down.

"I think we are wasting our opportunity," she said

once, and Euny looked fiercely at her and said, "Hold your tongue, child!" which at once lit a rebellious flame in Wise Child's eye.

A crisis came one afternoon when we were out in the field with the prince and Cormac. The prince had just galloped Golden himself—he was demonstrating some way of controlling the bay to Cormac—and had, of course, been shadowed by Meroot's soldiers. They always kept well out of his way, but they were unmistakably there watching him, ready to surround him if he went farther than the boundaries permitted him. He returned to us, slid off his horse, and watched Cormac mount Golden and ride away. I could sense his depression. "It should be me," he murmured under his breath.

"Then let it be," Wise Child suddenly said. "Ride the horse in the race. You could probably outgallop the soldiers, in any case. Your horse is much better than theirs!"

A look of anger crossed the prince's face. "Did Meroot send you to trap me?" he asked sharply.

The absolute astonishment of Wise Child was her best defense.

"How can you say such a thing? I see how you love to ride and how much you love Golden. Why should you not ride him on your birthday?"

"It would never be allowed, that's why!" He spoke shortly, and I could hear him breathing fast with anger.

"Don't let on that you are going to ride him," Wise

Child went on. "Pretend that Cormac is going to do it, and then at the last minute ride yourself. You will be gone before they can do anything."

"Are you mad?" asked the prince roughly. "I have to live here, do I not? What is worse, if I behave badly, the people of Castle Dore suffer. Did you know that? Every time I disobey Meroot, the people in the village are punished."

Wise Child was speechless for a few moments.

"That is terrible," she said. "I did not know that."

"And so"—the prince shrugged—"I am helpless. There is no way out of my situation."

Wise Child reported part of this conversation to Euny, leaving out the part where she had come close to inciting the prince to rebellion.

"Ah!" said Euny. "Another clue to the prince's frame of mind. You see how right I was to make you wait." Euny never minded being irritating or saying "I told you so."

Wise Child raised an eyebrow at me when Euny wasn't looking and shrugged dramatically.

"I think soon we will need to talk more frankly to the prince," Wise Child said, not prepared to let it go.

"Do you indeed?" replied Euny, and said no more.

What I could see very well was that if Wise Child had not exactly talked frankly to the prince, she had at least opened up a train of thought in him that he was bound to pursue. If we had been trying to work out whether we could trust the prince, now he, equally, must be wondering how far we were to be trusted.

Sure enough, our conversations began to include what I thought of as "fishing" lines lowered into the depths to elicit revealing answers.

"So what do you make of Meroot?" he asked one day.

"Powerful!" replied Wise Child, in a voice that could have been conveying admiration. "As a foreigner, I don't quite understand the situation, however. Why are you not ruling in your own kingdom? Why does she control the future king of Castle Dore? Or have I misunderstood something?"

"It's a long story," the prince said shortly. "But as I explained before, I have no choice."

Wise Child did not leave it at that.

"Do you *want* to rule your own kingdom?" she pushed. "I realize that you are very young and that kingship is a heavy responsibility, but when you are a bit older, perhaps?" Her apparent innocence was very convincing. It was as if she had no idea of the tragic history of Castle Dore.

The prince gave a groan but did not reply.

Before our next meeting, Wise Child primed me to push things a little further. With some trepidation, I agreed.

"So, after your birthday celebrations," I said, "will things start to change for you?"

The result was astonishing. It was as if I had, with my

fairly dull question, brought about a change in the prince, a landslide of emotion, though no doubt ever since we had started getting to know him, this moment of crisis had been approaching. His great dark eyes filled with anger, fear, and . . . hope? I could not tell.

"There is something going on here," he said in a strangled voice. "I don't know what it is. I don't know whether you are spies. I don't know what your game is!"

"We are your friends," said Wise Child quietly. "We are here to help you—you, not Meroot—in any way we can."

"Why?" he asked.

"We cannot tell you that at the moment, but trust us. No harm shall come to Castle Dore through us—or at least not if we can help it. We want to see Castle Dore restored, and you as its rightful king."

If I had doubted the essential goodness of Prince Brangwyn up till then, I knew at that moment that he was not Meroot's cat's-paw, that his hope, his ambition, his passion was to rule on his father's throne and to deliver his people.

There was a long silence. Then the prince said in a very small, humble voice, "I think I am going to have to trust you. I don't exactly know why, but I *do* trust you."

"Quite right!" said Wise Child in her most grown-up voice. "You won't regret it."

Carefully, we did not tell the prince about Finbar and

the arms (we did not feel that this was our secret to tell), but we told him that plans were afoot to bring about change. Though we were not at liberty to divulge the details, so far as possible, they would not risk the lives of his people.

"For goodness' sake, though," said Wise Child, "don't start looking more cheerful. Go on being sulky and miserable."

The prince laughed.

"Well, that's torn it!" said Wise Child as we marched back to Euny. "The cat's out of the bag now. I suppose I had better go and make a clean breast of it."

Naturally, I went with Wise Child and claimed an equal part in the revelation we had made to the prince. I was dreading the encounter because Euny, even in a good temper, was quite formidable. I could imagine that when she was angry, she might be terrifying. She did the oddest thing, however.

Wise Child, without a trace of penitence, poured out the story of what had been said. Instead of losing her temper or even uttering a rebuke, Euny burst out laughing.

"So the little girl knows better, does she?" she said, almost admiringly.

"Not so little!" said Wise Child.

"Well, you've done it now," said Euny. "Don't blame me if you end up in Meroot's dungeon. Don't expect *me* to lift a finger to save you."

"I certainly should expect it," said Wise Child, by now in a cheeky mood, "just as I would do what I could to save you."

Perhaps because Wise Child had taken charge in a way unexpected to Euny, Euny began to explain to us that Juniper would be coming to the castle for the birthday celebration and that the point of this would be a concentration of *doranic* powers.

"The combined effect of myself and Juniper will work like scales against the counter-magic of this dreadful place," said Euny.

"And, of course, my *doranic* powers, too," put in Wise Child.

"Maybe," said Euny, not denying it.

Around this time I began to have bad dreams. I would wake sweating on my hard pallet in the room adjoining Euny's and try to throw off the sense of fear. Usually the dream was about being pursued, sometimes by a shadow, sometimes by Meroot herself. You can imagine my concern when, suddenly, Meroot sent for me and Wise Child.

"She will see you in her workroom," said the footman who gave us her order. Euny herself was busy elsewhere in the castle, so we had no chance to discover whether she had arranged, or expected, this meeting. With sinking hearts, we found our way to Meroot's workroom. When the door opened, it was into a strangely dark room, with a number of tables holding mysterious objects—flasks of liquid, bundles of herbs, amulets hung from nails, a staff or two leaning against the wall. The deep shadows and the shape of the room, which was long and thin, gave it the sinister feeling of a cave. I noticed a rat nibbling at one of the bundles of herbs, and it eyed us with its hot, hostile glance. The room had an unpleasant smell. There was a huge fireplace with a fierce fire and a pot bubbling upon it. It gave out a noxious plume of smoke.

At first there was no sign of Meroot, and we waited in a frightened silence for some minutes. It may have been my imagination, but I thought I could hear groans and little cries of suffering from a huge cupboard that stood in a corner. Then Meroot emerged out of the dimness, leaning heavily on a stick. She sank into a large carved chair and pointed speechlessly with her stick to a couple of footstools, on which we quickly sat down.

"So how are the birthday preparations going?" Meroot asked. Her voice had so much habitual scorn in it that it was difficult to tell whether she was mocking us or whether this was just the way she usually talked. Wise Child, always readier with speech than myself, plunged into a description of Prince Brangwyn's orders and the people we had briefed to carry them out.

"And the prince?" said Meroot icily. "Is he looking forward to the celebration?"

"Very much!" lied Wise Child promptly. She is a

naturally truthful girl, but protecting the prince was our first concern.

"The prince seems to feel that he should be allowed to participate in the wrestling and fighting," Meroot said. "Of course, it is unthinkable for someone of his degree to demean himself in that way, or for that matter in the horse race. Someone might beat him, for example."

Wise Child nodded vigorously. Meroot watched her with her strange, light eyes, as concentrated as a cat watching a mouse. "That must not happen!" Wise Child said.

"You realize," said Meroot, "that if anything goes wrong with the preparations—*anything*—you will both be punished severely?"

"Quite right!" said Wise Child. "We must take responsibility, of course."

When we were outside again and on our way back to our room, I said to Wise Child, "Where are the protections?"

"I am wearing the silver moon, and I have the black egg and the cloth-of-disguise bottle in my pocket. I had to leave the flask behind because it is too big to carry."

"We are going to have to find a safer hiding place for it, maybe outside the castle."

Wise Child was sufficiently frightened by our encounter with Meroot to agree with me for once without argument, and she went at once to the cupboard in our room where the flask was carefully hidden, first behind a pile of candlesticks and odds and ends of candles, and then behind our few clothes.

"Wait! I know it's in here!" Wise Child swept the clothes out of the way and began removing the candle ends and the candlesticks.

"It's just at the back here. It's . . ." Her voice died away. "Colman, it isn't here!"

"She's found us out," I said. "She'll know it was a magical object."

We looked at each other with white, stricken faces. Not only had we lost a very precious protection given to us by the Mother, but, almost certainly, Meroot now suspected us. We tried to convince each other that someone else might have taken the flask—Euny, for example, or a servant sent to find a candlestick, or someone merely curious—but it was not easy to see why anyone who did not know its worth would want to steal a flask containing an unknown liquid.

To our huge relief Euny entered at that moment, and we poured it all out to her, our encounter with Meroot and the loss of the flask. It always took a lot to disconcert Euny, but she turned perceptibly paler and sat down rather quickly. None of us were in the least doubt of the potential cruelty of Meroot, and, of course, since Euny had employed us, she, too, might partake in our downfall.

"I must make an excuse to go and see Meroot," she said. "I will try to discover whether she suspects me, or whether she will tell me she suspects you of working against her. In the meantime, carry on as usual—you have little choice. Go to see Prince Brangwyn this afternoon. If you see an opportunity, push the conversation further—to the possibility of his escape. There is little to lose now, and this may be your last chance to talk to him. We none of us know what may happen in the next day and night. Keep up your courage and know that whatever happens, I will do my best to help you. I will try to find Cormac and tell him the details. With luck, it will not occur to Meroot to suspect him." And with that, Euny was gone. We felt fearful and alone without her.

Promptly, at our usual time, we presented ourselves to the prince. I could detect no change in him. Whatever Meroot was thinking, she had not shared her dark broodings with him. Wise Child scarcely even pretended to carry on a normal conversation. Within a few moments she was saying, "You may not see us again, sir. Meroot, we think, has decided that we are a danger to you."

The prince's eyes widened with surprise. "Why?"

"What you don't know about us is that we are friends of your lost sister, Ninnoc, whom I know as Juniper," Wise Child said. "I was trained by her in magic. We came here especially to try to help you—you and Castle Dore—and it is not too late to do so. Great forces of magic are gathering here on your behalf, and the people of Castle Dore may secretly rise against Caerleon, but for that to happen you need to escape and become their leader. They love and admire you still, would do anything for you. You must escape on horseback on the day of the race, outgallop all the other horsemen, and make your way to Castle Dore."

"What are you thinking of?" said the prince. "I shall be a marked man from the moment I get on the horse, and even if I get away, I will be followed back to Castle Dore. It is impossible."

"Not at all," Wise Child said. From her pocket she produced the glass bottle with the scrap of fabric. "I have here a magical protection called the cloth of disguise. If you and Cormac cut the cloth in half just before the race and carry half each, for a while he will appear to be you, and you will appear to be him, down to the very clothes you both stand up in. By the time Cormac begins to look like himself again, you will be well away, halfway back to Castle Dore."

"I don't believe it," said the prince.

"It is true," I said. "Unlikely as it sounds, it really works like that. What have you got to lose, anyway? If the spell does not work, you won't get farther than the end of the field. But if it does work, it gives you a chance to take on your own power."

The prince gazed at me with a terrifying intensity as I spoke, and then gave a sort of groan as the possibilities sank in. Wise Child handed him the little bottle, and as if this kind of thing were the most natural in the world, he carefully hid it in his robe. I found myself sighing with relief. That was one protection out of the way.

"I will do it," he said at last. "As you say, what is to be lost?" A silence fell among us, but it was an eloquent silence. We stared at one another, drawing comfort from one another's faces.

"Why now?" said the prince at last.

"We have reason to think Meroot suspects us," I said. "Which may mean that you will not see us again."

"That means you are in danger?"

"Yes, it does."

The prince groaned again. "In order to help me."

"And Castle Dore," Wise Child said. "And Juniper."

As if her comment had reminded him, the prince said, "Tell me about my sister. You know, I have not seen her for many years. She was young and beautiful when she left."

"She is still beautiful," said Wise Child, "and a woman full of power. So full of power that she was driven from her home by those who hated her, and she came here to ask for refuge."

"So where is she?"

"Not far away."

A tiny sound suddenly made me turn. Standing just inside the room was Meroot, with that horribly intent gaze that I found so troubling. How much had she overheard, I wondered.

"That will do," she said. "I think, Brangwyn, these children need not trouble you again. The preparations for your birthday are all but complete. Come with me," she said to us, and she pushed us in front of her through the door of Prince Brangwyn's room and closed it firmly behind her.

"We shall meet again very soon," she said ominously to us. "Meanwhile, go back to your room and stay there till I send for you."

Even as she spoke, I noticed a spasm pass through her as if she was in great pain. She struggled to get control of herself. "Go!" she said in a voice that turned into a gasp, and without waiting for further instructions, we fled.

We had hoped to find Euny in her room when we returned, but there was no sign of her. We hung around waiting, not daring to go away, even in search of supper, but still she did not come. This frightened us. Not only did we desperately need to share our encounter with Meroot with her, but we also feared that we had endangered Euny and that she, too, would now become an object of suspicion.

Finally we went to bed. Wise Child fell asleep almost at once, but I tossed and turned for what felt like hours, until I plunged into an exhausted sleep full of lurid dreams. In one of them I could see Meroot's eyes watching me through a window. For some reason, I was trying to stand between the window and Wise Child, who was with me in the room, so that Meroot would not know that Wise Child was there. There was a noise of shouting. A harsh voice was saying, "Get up, get up," and shaking me roughly.

Then, in horror, I realized that I *was* being shaken roughly, pulled and dragged out of bed. I forced myself awake, wrested myself free from the grasp that held me, and found that one of Meroot's huge soldiers was standing over me, shouting at me. I turned desperately to look for Wise Child, but her bed was empty.

"Get dressed!" the soldier shouted at me.

"Where is my friend?" I asked.

"None of your business. Get dressed!"

"Where is my friend? I won't get dressed until you tell me."

He knocked me down with a single blow.

"You will do what I tell you."

Pushing and prodding, he hurried me, more or less dressed, downstairs till we came to the part of the castle that I recognized as belonging to Meroot. He forced me into Meroot's workroom, where I was immensely relieved to see Wise Child standing alone, watched over by another huge soldier. We looked at each other in fear.

"They are bound to search us," Wise Child said to me in our own language. "What will Meroot say when she sees the silver moon and the black egg?"

"Where are they?" I asked.

"In the pocket of my coat. I dared not leave the egg behind, and I slipped the silver moon off on my way here."

Just then Meroot emerged, as she had done before, from the shadows of her dismal room. Euny accompanied her and carried the flask of purple liquid. Meroot looked much sicker. She was deathly pale, and her eyes seemed sunk in her head. I felt sure that I was looking at a woman gravely ill.

Euny at once began to scold us.

"I am appalled to learn that you appear to have abused my lady's hospitality," she said. "She was good enough to employ you, but it would seem that you had another purpose in coming here. She tells me that a magical object was found among your possessions."

"What magical object?" asked Wise Child.

"A flask of purple liquid. This flask here."

"It was given to us by a friend before we left home. We took it so as not to hurt her feelings. We had no idea what it was for."

It sounded a lame excuse.

"My lady believes that you have been plotting with the prince."

"Plotting what? We have come from Dalriada. We have no interest in the politics of Cornwall. We thought the prince was lonely and needed the company of young people, and we tried to cheer him up. We played chess with him, and I played the harp and sang to him, and we watched him race his horse."

It may appear that this was all said fluently by Wise Child, but this was not the case. The stress of the occasion did not help her use of Cornish. She stumbled badly over her words, hesitating, getting things wrong, mumbling, stopping and starting.

In the end Meroot stopped her and turned to Euny.

"I believe you told me you have traveled in Dalriada and can speak their appalling language," she said. "Tell them in words they can understand what they are accused of and what will be done to them if they do not confess."

"My lady Meroot regards you as traitors," Euny said icily in our own language, "and intends to have you confined in her dungeons until you confess. What I would like to know," she went on in the same stern and emphatic tone, "is whether you have any of the protections on you, and if so, where they are."

Wise Child, managing to sound rebellious, answered her.

"The silver moon and the egg—both are in my coat pocket."

"They refuse to confess, my lady," Euny said to Meroot in Cornish. "I think they need to be taught a lesson."

"Very well," said Meroot. "The soldiers shall take them to the small dungeon, search them, and leave them there for the night. I do not think they will need blankets or food. It is cold in the dungeon and that should help concentrate their minds."

"Quite right, my lady!" said Euny. "They won't need their coats, either." She leaned over and twitched Wise Child's coat away from her, and one of the soldiers wrenched my coat from my shoulders and threw it to Euny.

"I will see both of them in the morning," said Meroot, a world of venom in her tone.

"They deserve everything that's coming to them," said Euny viciously, tucking our coats under her arm as spitefully as if she had wished it was us she was holding. "How dare they abuse my lady's hospitality!"

I can barely describe our wretchedness that night. The soldiers hustled us down flights and flights of stairs where the air grew colder and colder and the feeling of being surrounded, weighed down, by stone became more and more oppressive. Worse, as we approached the dungeons, we could hear cries from the prisoners. As we drew nearer, we could see that Meroot and the knight had the prison cells made like cages with bars at the front. This gave the prisoners no privacy, not even the privacy of prison, but it also meant, it occurred to me, that Meroot could enjoy the sight of human creatures locked up like animals. She could feed off their despair and pain.

Finally we came to a small cell with a tiny window high up on one wall. The soldiers quickly searched us, then pushed us inside. The door clanged mercilessly behind us, and with much flourishing of keys, the soldiers locked it and went away, their footsteps echoing along the stone floors until we could hear them no longer. They had left us what was little more than a candle end to light us in this terrible place. There were two straw pallets with a thin blanket on each, one chair, and a bucket. The place smelled of damp, and it occurred to me that it was near the river.

With one accord we put our arms around each other.

"At least Euny has got the protections," Wise Child said.

"Which also means that we *haven't* got them," I pointed out. "Do you miss the silver moon?"

"I do," said Wise Child. "I feel sort of naked without it. And the egg was a comforting thing to hold in one's pocket." She paused. "Thank you for not saying 'I told you so,' for not pointing out the risks I was taking with the prince."

"But I'm sure the prince didn't betray us," I said. "It was just the frequency of our visits that made Meroot suspicious and search our things. She must have seen us that time in the hallway."

"Odd to think that it was one of the protections that gave us away," said Wise Child after a silence. "'The tools of the *doran*,' as they are known, do not usually work to bring a *doran* into danger. It makes me feel that something good must be going on that we don't know about."

"One good thing will be if the prince uses the cloth of disguise."

"Do you think he will? It's asking a lot of someone who does not know much about magic, even if he is the brother of a *doran*."

We were both tired after the terrors of the night, though also too stressed to sleep easily. We put the pallets side by side and lay down on them. They were hard, with some of the cold of the floor coming through.

"You do entirely believe in your vocation as a *doran*," I said to Wise Child. It was really a question, since thinking about *dorans* seemed one of the few possibilities of hope in our situation.

"Completely," she said. "For a while I wavered back there, after the trial and on that journey to Cornwall, but then the feeling bounced back stronger than ever." I found her certainty oddly comforting, although no opportunity to use her power presented itself.

"I'd give anything for a bite to eat," Wise Child said, echoing my own thoughts. Our meager supper seemed years away. As if one melancholy thought inspired another, after a bit she said, "They may torture us. In fact, knowing Meroot, she almost certainly will."

"I know." My stomach contracted with fear. "What mustn't we say?"

"Anything about Castle Dore."

"We shall have to confess to something, if only to look as if we are cooperating."

"Suppose we said we felt sorry for the prince, who did not seem very happy, and thought he should be allowed to take part in the horse race?"

"But it is the protection that will interest Meroot most. What is a *doran* doing at Caerleon? I cannot think of an answer to that."

Perhaps fear made us sleepy, because soon we were half asleep on our uncomfortable beds. We had left the candle alight—it was near to extinction anyway—and as it guttered, it threw weird shadows on the ceiling.

"Colman!" Wise Child suddenly hissed. "There's somebody coming!"

We could hear echoing footsteps descending the stairs, though the noise was not like the boots of soldiers.

"Not Meroot!" I said fervently.

"She's not well enough to cope with the steps," Wise Child said comfortingly, but all the same we waited nervously. Soon we could see the light of a lantern approaching.

Suddenly, to our amazement, we saw Euny. To our delight she produced a substantial pie and a flask of water, which she slipped between the bars of our cell.

"Eat all the pie, smash the flask when you have drunk the water, and hide the pieces in a dark corner," she said. "If the soldiers find it, they might suspect me. Meroot, partly because she depends on me to help her with her pain, still believes in me. I've also brought the silver moon and the black egg. I suggest that each of you conceals one of them about your person. They are unlikely to search you again."

"What are we to do, Euny?" Wise Child asked, her mouth full of pie.

"Play it as it comes, naturally," Euny said in no very sympathetic tone. "I will be around to help as much as I

can, but I don't envy you. Tomorrow may be rather nasty."
It was typical of Euny not to make things seem rosier than
they were.

"Trust in the power of the *dorans*," she added as an
afterthought.

"I do," said Wise Child. "But whether I will if I am
tortured . . ."

"Well, you'll find out, I expect," Euny said robustly.
"I must get back. I might be missed. I am doing what I can
to control the situation. Good night!" And with that she
was gone, leaving us in the dark.

Wise Child and I finished the pie and drank all the
water, then smashed the flask as Euny had instructed.

"Good night, Colman," Wise Child said after a
painful pause.

"Good night, Wise Child." It was a while before
either of us fell asleep. We lay dreading the morning.

CHAPTER ELEVEN

After her encounter with Euny, Juniper returned to Castle Dore. Finbar arrived soon thereafter. King Mark's gold had stimulated the Irish blacksmiths and silversmiths to fine feats of workmanship. In the hold of his ship he had stored many shields, helmets, breastplates, swords, and daggers. As soon as his ship was sighted in the bay, Lyon and the others sent out their smaller boats, loaded them with his cargo, and took the precious objects back to the Cave of the Mermaids.

When Finbar returned to Castle Dore, he was horrified that Juniper had let Wise Child run into danger, and with difficulty she restrained him from setting off to Caerleon at once to bring her home. Patiently she told him about the dreaming bundle, about Wise Child's determination to go, about Cormac's support of her, and about my belated decision to join them. And then, wondering if he would believe a word he heard, she told him about her meeting with Euny.

"Euny!" he said somewhat scornfully. He had never

forgiven her for the way she had once not given Juniper enough to eat and had subjected her to cold, discomfort, and worse.

"She's the one," said Juniper. "Never mind what you think of her. She's the one who is going to help us to save Castle Dore."

Juniper then told Finbar about Euny's instructions to her to go to Caerleon in disguise and her worries about it. It did not occur to her not to obey her old teacher, but she was hard put to think of a disguise that would not betray her immediately to her aunt Meroot. The very idea of a disguise was painful to her. She was accustomed to being herself.

"Treat it as a game," said Finbar. "Pretend that it is going to be fun. A chance to wear fancy dress."

"I don't think it would work if I went as a guest," Juniper replied thoughtfully. "They've probably counted the guests or else will want to know who they are. I could go as an entertainer, a singer or storyteller, perhaps."

"What do you feel about going back to Caerleon?" Finbar asked her curiously.

"Meroot frightens me less than the Gray Knight," Juniper replied. "But yes, Caerleon itself frightens me. I would not go there for anyone less than Euny. Or Wise Child."

"Who should never have been allowed to go there," put in Finbar.

"It is not so easy to stay a *doran* who has made up her mind," said Juniper.

"She is too young to be a *doran* or anything else."

"The *dorans* say that one is a *doran* from one's cradle," Juniper answered. "Sooner or later you have to recognize it, then train the natural skills that you have and be willing to become a *doran*. There is no doubt now that Wise Child is willing. When will you distribute the weapons to the villagers?" she asked.

"Not until absolutely necessary. It is too dangerous. When their original weapons were taken from them, one man, Ruan, kept his and hid them. A week later Perquin ordered a search of all the houses to make sure everyone had obeyed. Ruan's weapons were discovered. They tied him to a tree and impaled him with his own sword."

Juniper, who could remember Ruan from her childhood, looked stricken.

"I didn't know that. In that case, I'm amazed that anyone is prepared to take up weapons again."

"And I am amazed that no one has betrayed us to Perquin," Finbar said.

"They are good people here," said Juniper.

"But they mustn't be asked to run unnecessary risks. So long as the Cave of the Mermaids is unknown to Perquin, it is a safe place. When the time comes, all the men can go there and arm and set off together as the army of Castle Dore."

"What chance will they stand against the Gray Knight's men?"

Finbar looked mysterious. "It looks as if we shall not be alone."

"You *are* hiring mercenaries, you mean?"

"No need for that. It turns out that we have allies."

"Who?" Juniper asked in surprise.

"Castle Dore is not the only kingdom to suffer under the Gray Knight's oppression. The people of the Northland have also had their harvests stolen and their people persecuted. They are just as angry as the people here."

"So there will be two armies, even if they are rather small?"

"Maybe more. The Northlanders are trying to find other friends, and it is easier than you might think because people fear that sooner or later the Gray Knight will turn on them. So we shall have many men, I think, and we shall plan to take the castle by surprise. The only question is when."

"I have been meaning to tell you," Juniper said, "that Brangwyn has asked that Erc, the harpist, should go to the castle to play at his birthday celebration. A messenger came from Meroot inviting him, and we have told him that he must, of course, go. Erc may be able to get a message back to us."

"Erc is blind," said Finbar.

"And brave as a lion," Juniper said. "Because he is blind he is insisting on companions to go with him.

Brychan's sons, twin boys called Levan and Nectan, fifteen years old, have volunteered. Then one of them can come back with information."

Finbar brooded over the news that Brangwyn had asked specially for a harpist from Castle Dore. "Do you think it was an act of rebellion against Meroot?" he said. "It certainly suggests that he has not forgotten Castle Dore."

"And the people have not forgotten him," said Juniper. "He is their sign of hope. They are prepared to risk danger for him and for Castle Dore."

"As Wise Child is."

Finbar would have been more worried than he was if he had known the frightful situation in which Wise Child and I now found ourselves. Because of cold and discomfort I barely slept on that first night in the prison, but when I did at last fall into a troubled sleep, I was awakened by a disturbing sound. I soon knew what it was. Wise Child was very quietly crying. I don't know about anyone else, but I often hate people to know that I am crying. For this reason, I could not decide at first whether to let her know that I knew. But then a louder sob escaped her, and I could not bear it. I reached out and took her hand.

"We will get through this," I told her reassuringly.

"I think Meroot will kill us. After torturing us," said Wise Child, and then her tears could be contained no longer. "I am cold and hungry and frightened!" she said, her words ending in another sob.

"Listen!" I said, trying to sound more cheerful than I felt. "We have Euny on our side, and we have the protections, which must count for something. Somewhere around the castle is Cormac, who will help us if he can. All that apart, we have each other, and we are totally on each other's side."

Rack my brains as I might, I could not think of anything else to say. All the same, Wise Child cheered up a bit, as you often do when you have spoken about the things that frighten you most, even though none of them have changed.

"I know," she said. "It could be worse."

The light of morning was filtering into our horrible prison, revealing puddles on the floor and the cheerless walls of gray stone.

"I wonder what Prince Brangwyn thinks has become of us," I went on. "I wonder if he has mentioned us to Cormac."

A little later we could hear the sound of the soldiers' boots on the stairs, and we knew that they were coming for us. We squeezed hands, but by now we were quite calm. They pushed and hustled us—quite unnecessarily, since we were not resisting—and we climbed the innumerable steps to Meroot's workroom. This time she was seated in a large carved chair, with Euny standing beside her. The flask of purple liquid sat next to them on a table. The soldiers half threw us into the room, and we stood in front of Meroot.

She looked paler than ever, and as if her eyes were sunken into her head.

"You can leave us," she said to the men. My eyes were drawn to a brazier on one side of the room with a fierce fire burning in it. My knees started to shake. Surely Meroot would not . . . But I knew very well that there was nothing Meroot would not do if it suited her.

"So?" said Meroot in a rather faint voice. "You have tasted the hospitality of my dungeons. I trust it was to your liking?"

We said nothing.

"Of course, I could just leave you both there to rot, but I must confess that I am curious about you. You come here posing as two innocent children in search of work, and then I find that you are dabbling in magic. It is bad luck for you that I know something of magic. So perhaps you would care to tell me what sort of magic you were thinking of practicing here, and why?"

Neither of us could think of anything to say.

"Cat got your tongue? Oh, I think, don't you, Juliot, that we could persuade them to say a little more than that?"

Euny was silent. I thought that she looked strained and tired, something I never remembered noticing in her before.

Meroot got up slowly and awkwardly from her chair; then, walking across the room, she picked up a long metal rod that was leaning against the wall. She thrust it into the heart of the brazier, where almost at once it became rosy red and then white-hot.

"Fire," said Meroot thoughtfully. "It never fails to make people speak."

Wise Child and I watched the rod become hotter and hotter, as if hypnotized.

"Or should we see what another day of hunger and thirst might achieve?" asked Meroot. "Juliot, what do you think?"

"I have an idea that I would like to put to my lady in private," Euny replied.

"Very well," said Meroot, surprised. "But it had better be a good one."

We were bundled outside to wait on this conversation. We heard their voices rising and falling for a while, and then Meroot summoned us again.

"This afternoon," she said, "I wish you to go and amuse Prince Brangwyn as usual. In the meantime, you can return to your cell."

It was only after we had got away from that horrible room that we fully understood how terrified we had been. My legs began to shake so much that I could barely walk downstairs, and even when we were back in the cell, we did not speak for some minutes.

"What is going on?" said Wise Child after a while. "I don't understand it."

"Meroot is certainly not concerned for us," I replied.

"It must be about trying to learn something of Prince Brangwyn's feelings. I bet she is going to plant someone in the room to eavesdrop."

"Put someone behind the tapestry, you mean? How horrible! To use us to lead the poor prince into trouble."

I nodded. "And we won't be able to warn him, or they will overhear."

We sat shivering in the cold cell until once again we were summoned, not by Euny as we had half hoped, but by the soldiers. Dirty and disheveled from our night in the cell, we were ushered into Prince Brangwyn's presence, where a surprise waited for us. Cormac stood beside the prince's chair.

The prince looked at our dirty, crumpled clothes in astonishment. We had never before presented ourselves to him in this condition. Also, something of the fear and distress we had endured must have shown on our faces. His habitual politeness fortunately took over and he did not ask questions, but I felt his glance upon us more than once and noted the slight frown on his face, as if he was working out the significance of it. With his natural courtesy, he offered us cakes and wine, which we gratefully accepted, and since we were both desperately hungry, we made short work of them. I felt that the prince was observing this, too. I could tell that Cormac was puzzling over our appearance, looking at us with that special quality of concern that was all his own.

"Is everything all right?" the prince asked gently.

"Yes, yes," said Wise Child, almost impatiently. She was glancing round the room to see where a potential eavesdropper might be hidden. I had already noticed a slight movement of the tapestry, which might have been a draft, but equally might have been a hidden eavesdropper. Cormac's presence was an advantage. I did not think that the prince would speak very frankly in front of him, even though he knew him to be a friend of ours.

It soon appeared, however, that he had merely obeyed a request from the prince to discuss some detail of Golden's care, some medicine the horse needed—the prince trusted Cormac more than he trusted Meroot's grooms—and that at any moment he might leave. I tried desperately to think of a way to keep him there. In the meantime, however, Wise Child, often quicker than me, had thought of a way of warning Brangwyn. The prince's poetry slate lay on a side table. Wise Child picked it up, as if curious about it, and, to the prince's astonishment and perhaps even anger, began to write.

TAKE CARE. EAVESDROPPER.

"There!" she said to the prince "I have found a rhyme for your poem," and she held out the slate to him.

A change came over his face as he read, but with his usual self-mastery, he said at once, "That's a better rhyme than I had thought of. It is you that should be the poet."

Wise Child took a piece of cloth and rubbed out the

words she had written. "It was just a passing thought," she said.

My fear was that the prince would be so angry at the thought of an intruder that he would at once pull back the tapestries to reveal him, but with his usual admirable self-control, he did nothing. Having dismissed Cormac, he began to talk casually to us about Golden, and then he asked Wise Child for a game of chess.

"Play my lute, if you wish," he said politely to me. He knew that I enjoyed picking out tunes and could do it rather well. In that warm, comfortable room, where everything appeared safe, it was difficult to believe in our damp prison—it felt like another world—and yet there seemed no hope of not having to return to it and to the worse horrors of Meroot's workroom. I longed to be able to tell the prince what had happened to us. I thought miserably that this might be the last good time we would ever know.

The game of chess seemed to move remarkably slowly. Wise Child, usually a rather impulsive player, deliberated for long periods over her moves—she told me later that she was brooding on whether there was anything she could do—and the prince started to doodle on his slate. I positioned myself between him and the tapestry as I played the lute—we did not know whether the eavesdropper could see as well as hear. The prince showed Wise Child the words he had written.

WHAT IS WRONG?

Hidden by my presence, and trying not to let the slate squeak, Wise Child wrote M. IS KEEPING US IN PRISON.

The prince picked up the cloth Wise Child had used and casually obliterated her words.

"Not a bad idea," he said. Then he went on, "We shan't finish this game today, Wise Child. Come back tomorrow, and I shall beat you hollow."

"No chance!" said Wise Child, but she looked more cheerful. If we did not return tomorrow, the prince would have reason to ask why.

The afternoon wore away until one of the soldiers came for us and we were escorted back to the deadly cold of the cell. With one accord we lay down on our pallets and covered ourselves with our meager blankets. There seemed nothing to say except, "You know, I am sure someone was hiding behind the tapestry. It moved several times."

"Once I thought I could hear breathing."

Both of us knew very well that late that night we would find ourselves back in Meroot's room, and we lay there waiting for the dread summons. I dozed off once or twice. I think it was a response to the sheer terror of our situation. Although Wise Child had saved the prince, it seemed as if nothing could save us.

The summons came. On legs from which all the strength seemed to have drained, we climbed the stairs. The room was much as it had been the night before, with the metal rod heating in the brazier and the flask of purple liquid laid out on the table as if in accusation.

Meroot's face seemed more sunken than it did the night before, her pale eyes uncanny against her ashen skin. Her hand on her snake stick trembled, I noticed. Once again Euny, looking very grave, stood beside her.

"You!" she said sharply, pointing her stick at Wise Child. "Step forward!"

Wise Child did so, slowly, reluctantly.

"So tell me about your practice of magic. What do you actually do?"

"I don't know what you mean."

"Oh, I think you do. No one who does not practice magic has a flask in their cupboard like that one."

"I told you." I could hear the tremble in Wise Child's voice. "I was looking after it for a friend."

"What friend? Someone in this house?"

"No. Someone I knew before I came here."

"Lies!" said Meroot fiercely. "All lies! So I am going to have to work for a confession then, am I?"

I could see that Wise Child held her hand to her breast, where the silver moon must be, and I wondered if it was growing hot, as it did when danger threatened. If it was going to protect her, then now was the moment.

"Juliot!" snapped Meroot. "Come here and hold the child." Meroot stood up with great difficulty and moved to the brazier, where, using a cloth, she took hold of the metal rod by the end and thrust it farther into the heart of the fire. She seemed strangely excited. I could see that her hands were trembling, and her face, so pale a few moments before, was flushed. Suddenly she let go of the metal rod and stumbled for a moment.

"My lady!" said Euny in apparent concern. "Sit down for a moment, and then you can give the child what she deserves."

Euny helped Meroot back to the carved chair, where she sat shaking, her hand over her face.

"I will get you a little wine, my lady," Euny said. "That will make you feel better." Euny moved into the shadows of Meroot's workroom, taking the purple flask with her. She returned with a goblet full of wine, but without the flask. She carried the goblet to Meroot, who drank the wine down in quick gulps.

"There, my lady, that will make you feel better!" Meroot's eyes rolled for a moment, and then suddenly she became quite still, her eyes closed, her body rigid in her chair.

"That will last for several hours," Euny told us, "during which time she will see and hear nothing."

"Won't she suspect you when she wakes up?" Wise Child asked.

"No, she won't remember anything about it. I will tell her that she fainted, and that I sent you both back to your cell."

As she spoke, Euny retrieved the now empty flask and

began to fill it with wine from one of Meroot's bottles. The liquid was not quite the same color, but I thought it was probably close enough to convince someone who had not just seen what had happened.

"Please help us, Euny," said Wise Child. "We are terrified of what Meroot will do to us."

"For heaven's sake!" said Euny, as if Wise Child were being utterly unreasonable. "You have just seen what the protections can do for you. Now concentrate, and I will tell you what will happen next. Soon I will ask the soldiers to take you back to your cell. They will lock you in, and therefore be able to confirm to Meroot that they did so. Later, while it is still dark, Cormac will come and release you and will take you to his room, where he will hide you until the day of the feast."

Euny put her hand in among her many garments, felt in some inner pocket, and produced a key, which she handed to me.

"Keep it where it cannot be seen," she said unnecessarily.

"Won't Meroot suspect you when she knows we've escaped?" Wise Child asked.

"Possibly, but probably not. She does not know that I have a key to the prison, and I will be so indignant about your escape that it will be hard for her to believe that I am in league with you. Is there anything else that you need to know?"

"What is going to happen on the day of the feast?" Wise Child said. "That's what we need to know."

"None of your business, child," Euny said infuriatingly.

"Yes, it is my business," Wise Child said emphatically, drawing herself up in her dirty, disheveled clothes and looking Euny square in the eye. "I am part of the power of the *dorans* in this place, and I can only use my power if I know what is going on, so don't treat me like a child."

I could see a flicker of surprise on Euny's face. She was silent for a moment, and then, like one defeated in argument, said, with unusual grace for her, "You are right. If I knew more, I would tell you more. All I know at present is that Juniper will come to the feast—I have commanded her to do so. That Prince Brangwyn, thanks to your efforts, will probably ride in the birthday race. And that if Finbar can accomplish it, the men of Castle Dore will attack Caerleon. That is all I can tell you. The rest depends on the *doran* secret—the ability to work in harmony with events, not oppose them, with our willpower."

The two *dorans*—Euny, with a lifetime of experience behind her, and Wise Child, little more than a child—stood and continued to stare at each other, both of them, I thought, as if they were seeing the other properly for the first time. It was Wise Child who broke the long silence that fell between them.

"Very well," she said, with that special air of authority she could assume sometimes that made her seem not like a child at all. "You have answered my question. Call the soldiers and let us go back to our cell. I will try to trust in the protections to carry us through."

As before, we were pushed and prodded down the stairs and into our cell. When the soldiers had gone, I pulled out the key and tried it in the door. Although I trusted Euny on the whole, it was difficult to believe it would work, but it did—the door swung smoothly open.

Knowing we could get out of the cell, not to mention the conversation we had had with Euny, made both of us feel much more cheerful, although we were still miserably hungry and the bitter cold of the cell soon bit into our flesh.

"I hope Cormac comes soon," said Wise Child. "Wouldn't it be awful if Meroot woke up before he came and dragged us back to the workroom?"

"Somehow I don't think Euny would get that wrong," I said.

Time did hang very heavy on our hands, though. Every tiny sound—the drip of water, the scamper of rats, faraway voices, the distant cries and groans of other prisoners—strained our nerves. Although we lay down on our pallets for lack of anywhere else to sit, there was no question of sleep. We were horribly alert.

Our joy when Cormac's kind, scarred face appeared in front of our cell was immense. We had not heard him come—he had thought to wear a pair of felt slippers, the sort that Meroot, who had terrible headaches, often made her servants wear. He was carrying a club. His face was grave.

"We have to pass two guards at the head of the stairs," he said. "Euny thought they went off duty at night, but apparently not. They were asleep when I came down, but they may be awake by now. There is no way we can get to my room without passing them. If necessary, I shall have to hit them with my club."

We climbed the stairs up from the dungeons with a despairing feeling that we were going to get caught. Wise Child, I noticed, clutched the silver moon hidden under her clothes. Cormac pulled a hood over his head so that his face was hidden in shadow. We could hear the sound of snores before we reached the soldiers, and we tiptoed past the first of them. With a grunt and a shudder, the second soldier woke up and stared at us, stupefied by sleep.

"Here! Where do you think you're going?" he asked.

"The mistress has asked to see these two," Cormac replied promptly. "She's keen to make them talk, and she's going to use the fire to do it."

"Quite right!" said the soldier, still sleepy.

"Teach them a lesson they'll never forget," added Cormac. He ushered us round the corner and up the next flight of stairs and then said, "Run! As fast as you can!"

As if Cormac had anticipated what was about to follow, there was a shout from below. We could hear the sound of footsteps rapidly mounting the stairs, and following Cormac, we raced onward and upward, passing many turnings but eventually entering a dark passage. There we hid behind a cupboard and were thankful to hear the soldiers rush past. We moved on down the passage, entering a maze of other passages, until suddenly Cormac opened a door into a tiny room that contained nothing but a bed, a chair, and a table. There was bread and a flask of water on the table, and, starving and thirsty as we were, he let us divide the bread and take turns drinking from his flask. Satisfied at last, Wise Child and I sank down on the bed and looked at Cormac.

"You risked a lot for us," Wise Child said. "Fortunately, I don't think the soldiers could recognize you if they saw you again. One thing, though. Having seen us in the presence of a footman, won't Meroot have all the rooms of the footmen searched?"

Cormac nodded.

"I've got an answer to that," he said. "There's a hiding place here, which I think you may need to use at least until the first hue and cry dies down." He pulled away a dirty, shabby rug that lay on the floor. I thought perhaps it would reveal a trapdoor, but there was no sign of any break in the floor. Cormac placed his knife to the side of one of the floorboards and gently eased it up. Then he removed another and another, and soon we could see a room, not entirely dark, beneath us. Cormac balanced on his arms, then lowered himself into the hole and gradually disappeared, dropping the last few feet.

"Now you come and I'll catch you," he said. First Wise Child, and then I, followed him. We found ourselves in a small chamber. In one wall was a slanting window. "Look there!" said Cormac. We looked and were astonished to find that we were looking into the Great Hall from a considerable height.

"My guess is that someone used this room to spy on the Great Hall," Cormac said. "Perhaps it was part of a room that belonged to the lady of the house. If she did not wish to sit at supper with the lord and his knights, she could watch the party from up here. Perhaps it was a way of seeing that he behaved himself, that he did not get too drunk or embrace other ladies. Anyway, at some point the room must have been built over. As far as I know, no one knows that it is here. I only discovered it by chance myself. It is not very comfortable, but it will make a good hiding place."

"It will," said Wise Child. "We shall be safe, and a great deal more at ease than we were in that hateful dungeon."

"I shall bring you food," said Cormac, "and do my best to make you comfortable." He had already placed a few cushions on the floor in readiness for our stay.

"Cormac, you are the greatest dear in the world," said Wise Child. "You have risked your life to save us and found us this wonderful place to hide." She impulsively hugged him and kissed him warmly on the cheek, and I could see that Cormac, for whom Wise Child could do no wrong, was delighted.

"Let us hope the time will soon come when there will be no more need to hide," he said.

"Or to be afraid," I said.

CHAPTER TWELVE

It was now two days to the feast. Perched in our strange little aerie, Wise Child and I watched the preparations begin in the hall below. We saw footmen, including Cormac, place fresh candles in the sconces and give the tables another scrubbing. They laid each place with its knife and its tankard for beer or wine. We thought—but this may just have been our hunger, which was barely appeased by the scraps Cormac was able to bring us—that we could smell the roasting of meat—the swans, wildfowl, boar, and oxen with which Prince Brangwyn's birthday was to be celebrated. Once the prince himself entered the hall, accompanied by the Gray Knight, and we craned our necks to try to gauge his expression.

"He looks sad," Wise Child said at last, and I agreed with her. We wondered what explanation he had been given for our disappearance. That Meroot had conducted a search for us throughout the castle we knew very well. On the morning after Cormac had spirited us away from our cell, we had heard shouting, the moving of furniture, and the tramp of many booted feet overhead. We guessed, rightly, that the soldiers were searching for us room by room. We trembled in our little chamber under Cormac's floor, and when we heard the boots directly above us, we clutched each other in terror, Wise Child uncharacteristically hiding her face on my shoulder. I could feel her shaking with fear. But then, to our huge relief, the sound of the feet retreated, and we both breathed again.

"We've done it!" I said triumphantly. We did not discuss the fact that we had no idea how we would ever escape from Cormac's room, nor what the outcome of all our efforts—Finbar's, Juniper's, Euny's—could possibly be. It was enough to live day by day, moment by moment.

There was another frightening episode when we saw a number of men, all footmen, lined up below us in the hall.

"Look," said Wise Child. "There's Cormac!"

We soon realized what the purpose was. Two soldiers, whom we recognized as the guards who had stopped us the night before, walked slowly along the line of men.

"They're trying to identify Cormac!" Wise Child said in dread. The soldiers walked up and down, peering closely into men's faces, but we were thankful to see that they barely glanced at Cormac and had no idea he was their quarry.

"Thank God for that!" I breathed when they passed him for the third time.

He came to see us later. He had brought us more

cushions and blankets, food and drink, and news of what was going on in the castle.

"Meroot is said to be furious, but she is keeping to her room," he told us. "She is issuing all kinds of threats to the soldiers about what she will do to them if they do not find you, so they are searching frantically in every nook and cranny of the castle."

"I wouldn't want to be in their shoes," said Wise Child with feeling.

"Tomorrow the guests start to arrive," Cormac told us. "There will be dinner tomorrow night, with songs and storytellers to keep the first guests happy, then the birthday proper begins the next day. In the afternoon will be the horse race. The morning after will be the crowning of the prince as *regulus*—this is Meroot's excuse for not letting the prince ride in the race himself. She says he might be injured. Then directly after the crowning comes the feast, which will go on for several days."

He paused. "It is rather puzzling," he went on. "Sometimes the prince talks as if I am to ride Golden in the race, sometimes as if he is going to. I wonder if he is quite right in his mind."

Wise Child and I exchanged glances and came to a wordless agreement. Swiftly Wise Child told him of the suggestion she had made to the prince, the deception it would involve in using the cloth of disguise, and the idea that the prince should escape and return to Castle Dore.

"For a while, as the cloth works, it will appear that you are the prince, and the prince, who will be riding Golden, is you."

"How long will the disguise work for?" Cormac asked.

"Until the prince discards his part of the cloth," Wise Child said. "Which means when he gets near to Castle Dore and needs the people to recognize him. On a fast horse like Golden, he should be there during the evening of the crowning day, when everyone is sitting at the feast. What it means, Cormac, is that you will be Prince Brangwyn both at the crowning and at the birthday feast. Maybe you should make an excuse as it gets late, and leave the Great Hall before you change back into being Cormac. Though it will seem odd if you leave your own feast before the end."

She added thoughtfully, "That apart, won't the prince's groom wonder about what became of Golden after the race?"

Cormac said, "I heard the prince tell them that tonight and tomorrow night he will stable him himself in Meroot's stable, as he may need special care after the race, and he and I can keep an eye on him there. The prince's groom does not go there."

As Wise Child explained this, it occurred to me that Cormac might be very angry, feeling that we had used him as a tool and put him in danger without ever asking his consent. It was a measure of Cormac's goodness, and his love for Wise Child, that he seemed to mind not at all, though he did have some worries.

"It's wonderful," he said, "to think of the prince returning to Castle Dore, and I am so pleased I can help him. But I have no idea how a prince should behave. 'Specially at a crowning. It is terrifying. Suppose I give the game away?"

"People see what they expect to see," Wise Child said sagely. "Almost anything you do will seem all right to them. Just look confident, pleased with yourself."

"Will they be expecting the prince when he gets to Castle Dore?" Cormac went on to ask.

"Euny says that they will, that a message will reach them, and Finbar will arm the men. Then they will march on Caerleon."

Cormac frowned. "Do you think those sad men can hold their own here?"

"I don't know," said Wise Child honestly. "They will at least be helped by the magic of three *dorans*—Euny, Juniper, and me—but Euny thinks Finbar may have other plans up his sleeve."

"Juniper!" said Cormac in surprise. "Juniper is coming here?"

"So Euny says, and she always knows everything."

We could see that Cormac found this a comforting thought.

"Have you seen Euny this morning?" I asked him. "I

keep worrying that Meroot will think our disappearance is her doing."

"I haven't seen her, but I suspect Euny can look after herself."

As if our question had prompted her appearance, a little later we observed Euny down below, ordering and scolding in her most high-handed fashion as she supervised the laying of fresh rushes on the floor and bunches of sweet-smelling herbs on the table where Meroot and the Gray Knight would sit with the grander guests. The high table stood on a raised platform, and two large carved chairs, looking rather like thrones, were placed in the middle. To the right of the larger chair was another carved chair, which I assumed was intended for the prince.

Apart from our observations of the flurries of activity down below, time passed slowly in our hiding place. We were much more comfortable than we had been in the dungeon, and Cormac fed us as well as he could with odd legs of chicken and hunks of bread he had managed to steal in the course of his duties. Yet our uncertainties about what was to come and what our own part in the events was likely to be kept us anxious, and what with that and the lack of exercise, we both slept badly. We discussed with Cormac whether it was worth taking the risk of spending time in his room rather than in our hiding place, but we both feared Meroot might order another search at any moment, and that we might get taken unawares.

"I cannot see how we can ever get out of here," Wise Child said gloomily at one point. "Meroot, or the soldiers, have only to recognize us, and we're done for."

I could not think of anything reassuring to say in reply.

We spent hours trying to work out what might be happening back at Castle Dore. Had Finbar armed the men yet? And where was Juniper?

That second night in our aerie we were entertained by the arrival of the first guests, who were to be given a modest dinner in the hall.

"Look!" said Wise Child. "There is a blind harpist— that must be Erc."

Erc was being guided by a handsome boy, and close behind him was another boy, identical in size and appearance. Also with the party was a woman wearing a wimple and a scarlet gown.

Erc tuned his harp and practiced a little, the boys and the woman sitting beside him. Other entertainers were also practicing—a juggler, a conjurer, and an acrobat, who did a number of astonishing somersaults between the tables.

By the time the diners arrived, about twenty in all, Erc was playing. He played some quiet music as the diners took their seats and began to eat. Then Erc played the introduction to a song, and the woman with the scarlet dress stood up and began to sing an old Cornish ballad. I felt Wise Child grow tense beside me.

"It's Juniper!" she gasped.

I stared hard at the woman, who seemed to me to bear little resemblance to Juniper.

"I'd know that voice anywhere," Wise Child said.

"She doesn't look much, if at all, like Juniper," I said doubtfully.

"You are used to seeing her with her hair loose. In any case, she must have used magic to make herself less recognizable."

I stared hard at the singer. Was she Juniper? I was far from sure.

"It's her voice, I tell you," said Wise Child obstinately. "I would know it anywhere."

The scent of the hot meat was very tempting to Wise Child and me with nothing but bread and a little cold chicken to dine on. Prince Brangwyn, Meroot, and the Gray Knight arrived and took their places at table. If Meroot had looked ill when we had last seen her in the workroom, she now looked ghastly. She tottered as she walked, even with the help of the knight on one side and her snake stick on the other. Her face had a yellow tinge, and her eyes seemed sunken and dead within her face. Once I saw her clutch her side as if in mortal pain. Euny walked a pace or two behind her, and I saw her take her place behind her chair. Once, when Meroot half-turned to her, Euny handed her a bottle, which Meroot smelled.

Prince Brangwyn, beautifully dressed in silk and linen,

had a moody look on his face, as if the last place he wanted to be was here. He ate listlessly and drank, I noticed, not at all. This made me think that he did intend to race Golden the next day. He did not look like a man who was soon to celebrate his birthday. At one point, however, he spotted Erc, leaped up from the table, and went to speak to him, and for the first time his face became animated. Meroot's eyes followed him, plainly suspicious.

In addition to the party at the high table, we were fascinated by the other guests. Nearly all of them were men, with only one or two ladies among them—the wives, we guessed, of some of the more important *reguli* and chieftains. Erc played throughout the meal, and the juggler amused the guests with astonishing feats with balls, and later with knives and forks.

At one point the woman with the scarlet dress sang again, a French song this time. Once again Wise Child became rigid. "How I wish I could talk to her!" Wise Child moaned. "It's awful to be so near to her."

I was still not sure that it was Juniper we were watching. We both kept our eyes on Meroot, knowing how dangerous it would be if she recognized her, but her eyes passed casually over the singer and back again to the food she was scarcely bothering to eat. The guests ate a delicious looking syllabub ("Oh, the cream!" moaned Wise Child).

Both of us slept very little that night. Early in the morning the servants were back, scrubbing the tables and making sure that all was in order. I imagined the frenzy in the kitchens, as the cooks labored ceaselessly at the spits, knowing well how unforgiving Meroot would be if anything went wrong.

We were in agony that day thinking of the moment when, we hoped, Prince Brangwyn, disguised as Cormac, would mount Golden and gallop away, not to win the race but to find his way back to Castle Dore. We would know that this had happened because Cormac, looking like the prince, would return to the room when he had the opportunity.

The day wore on, and there was no sign of Cormac. We speculated about what could have happened. Maybe the prince, never very sure about the use of the cloth of disguise and perhaps fearful of the outcome of using it, had decided to let Cormac race on Golden after all. Maybe the cloth had not worked, the prince had been stopped, and both he and Cormac were in trouble with Meroot. Maybe, the most terrible possibility of all, intimidated by the disappearance of Wise Child and myself, the prince had confessed all to Meroot.

"Well, I don't believe that one," Wise Child said stoutly. "Despite all that has happened to him, the prince strikes me as a brave man. He is Juniper's brother, after all."

She could not think of a better recommendation than that.

We clutched each other as we heard the door of

Cormac's room above us open and close, and a few moments later we were looking up into the face of Prince Brangwyn! Although we had half expected this transformation, it was still a weird surprise.

"What happened?" we breathed, trying to remember that it was Cormac we were talking to. "We expected you before this."

"The cloth of disguise worked perfectly," Cormac told us—in Prince Brangwyn's voice! He lowered himself into our hiding place. "I was wearing the colored suit that carries the prince's emblem; he was dressed as usual—well, as I am now. He used the cloth, and that was it! He had become me. I could tell, from looking down, that I had become him, but it was not until I looked at my reflection in the stable pond that I really believed it. I accompanied him to the field, gave him a leg-up, as the prince always does for me, and watched the start of the race. Then I noticed Meroot eyeing me. To my horror she came over and asked me to accompany her to her private apartment.

"I stood still until Golden had disappeared from view, and then could think of no excuse not to do as she asked. Of course, my fear was that my Cornish could never be mistaken for that of the prince. I started by merely grunting responses to what she said. She did not seem surprised, so I guess she was used to the prince being surly with her. Finally she asked me a direct question, and I felt that at any moment I would be unmasked. Then, to my astonishment and delight, as I framed the words in my broken Cornish, they corrected themselves in my mouth and came out fluently in that beautiful, confident way that the prince speaks! It was odd, but I felt as if I really *was* the prince."

"I wonder if he feels he is you?" Wise Child said. "Won't it feel odd to change back to your real selves!"

"That is the tricky bit," Cormac answered. "I don't like the feeling that as I return to being me, I shall get caught sitting at Meroot's high table. Quite apart from the terrors of the crowning tomorrow, I was not brought up to the high life. Though I have told the prince," he said evenly, "that he is not to think of that. He must discard the cloth whenever he needs to, and I will deal with what happens as best I can. It is vitally important that he discloses himself to his people as soon as possible."

"It is a huge risk for you to run," said Wise Child. "Why not just stay away from the feast? Pretend you are ill?"

"Do you think Meroot would allow that when I am the guest of honor? In any case, she has plans that I shall never leave her side all day tomorrow. No, I must see it through. If I disappear, she might get suspicious. She must not have any idea that Prince Brangwyn has returned home."

"You are a brave man," I said.

"I hope so," said Cormac. "I do not mind too much what happens if we can free the people of Castle Dore from their submission to Caerleon. It is also perfectly possible that Prince Brangwyn will not reach Castle Dore until much later, by which time I shall have made my excuses and gone to bed."

"What's it like being somebody else?" Wise Child asked curiously.

Cormac hesitated. "It's not just being somebody else," he said finally. "It is somebody else who is handsome as well as young. It makes a difference to have a face that people admire, rather than one that alarms them or arouses their curiosity."

Wise Child looked at him with the loving sympathy of which she was so capable.

"I hadn't thought of that," she said. "That must be hard."

"It *will* be hard," Cormac said, "when I revert to being myself again. At present it is rather exciting."

He did not stay long with us. He needed to get back to Prince Brangwyn's apartment before he was missed. We thought it unlikely we would talk to him again before the birthday feast.

That night Prince Brangwyn took his place with grace in the Great Hall. Erc and the Juniper-lady, as we called her, played and sang an old French song. ("She used to sing that to me in the white house!" Wise Child exclaimed in excitement.) The acrobats and conjurer amused the guests, and once again we watched and envied them their lovely food.

Erc, we noticed, was accompanied now by only *one* of the beautiful twins.

"I've been thinking," I said to Wise Child. "Sooner or later we have got to get out of this place, particularly if, God forbid, anything awful happens to Cormac. I cannot begin to think how we can do it safely. Even if the castle is attacked by Finbar and the others, it will still not be safe for us to emerge. A siege could go on for weeks, and if Cormac is discovered, we will have nothing to eat."

"I know," Wise Child said. "Apart from the silver crescent, we still have one of the protections—the black egg. I suppose we might use it to make our escape, but it would be awfully difficult to do."

We were silent for a long while after that.

"Well," said Wise Child at last, "at least at the moment we are not in that awful prison cell or being threatened with torture by Meroot. We just have to live with what is going on at the moment and not think too far ahead. The future is too frightening."

That day and night, with no visit from Cormac, seemed interminable. On the morning of the next day—his eighteenth birthday—Prince Brangwyn was to be proclaimed the official *regulus* of Cornwall, a horrible mockery for one who had no power at all and was not even allowed to go out without guards.

"At least the real prince is spared that," I said.

After a time we could hear shouting in the distance

and guessed that it was the traditional hailing of the new king by his neighbors.

"Hail King Brangwyn!" Wise Child said ironically.

At last the long afternoon crawled to a close, and the Great Hall began to fill again with the guests who had attended the crowning. All of them stood as the false King Brangwyn, wearing the small golden crown of the *regulus* that had belonged to King Mark, entered with Meroot and the Gray Knight. There was a round of applause from the guests, a shouting of the word "Hail!" and then there was special music sung by boys praising the new king's excellent qualities. As at the previous feast, Euny took up her station behind Meroot, who once again looked desperately ill. Soon a very grand feast began to be served, with servants carrying in huge platters of boar and swan.

"Look!" said Wise Child. "Do you notice how the Juniper-lady keeps eyeing Cormac? She knows that there is something different about him. It *must* be Juniper."

"Juniper has scarcely seen her brother since he was a baby. How would she know if he was different?"

"I have no idea, but it wouldn't surprise me if she did."

"Do you notice, only one of the twins is here again?" I pointed out.

And then it happened. Meroot was leaning to her right, listening to the new king, when suddenly she turned and glanced at him. I do not know whether he had suddenly started to talk in broken Cornish, or whether his speech became hard to understand, as it often did. Whatever it was, as she stared he began to change before her, and our, eyes. One moment he looked like both Brangwyn and Cormac simultaneously—it was the oddest thing—and then, quite swiftly and unmistakably, he was Cormac again.

Cormac and Meroot eyed each other in a kind of mutual terror. Meroot's eyes seemed to bulge for a moment and her face became ashen, and then suddenly she stood up, clutched herself, and fell forward across the table.

The whole hall became silent. Everyone stopped eating and stared in shock at the fallen body of Meroot. Cormac, quick as thought, slipped out of his chair and stood behind Meroot's, beside Euny, as if he were a servant.

Euny bent over Meroot, then said some words to the Gray Knight. The Gray Knight signaled to Cormac, just as if he had been there all along, to carry Meroot out of the hall. (Grand people scarcely notice their servants—they are simply there for their convenience—which made things safer for Cormac.) He followed, and Euny followed him.

Awkward, embarrassed by what had happened, the guests sat silent, not liking to eat. Nobody seemed to notice the fact that the young king had disappeared.

"Now what?" I said.

As if in answer to my question, Euny returned to the hall. She made a brief speech on behalf of her mistress, telling the guests that she had been taken ill, that she was attended by the Gray Knight and King Brangwyn, but that she wished them to continue to enjoy themselves. Glancing at one another, the guests slowly took up their knives, and a hubbub of talk broke out.

Having finished her speech and being once again ignored by the guests, Euny began making hand signals. Incredibly, we believed they were directed at us! The guests, if any of them noticed her, must have wondered what on earth she was doing, waving her hands in the air. Perhaps they thought it was some way of directing the footmen. But her meaning was quite clear to us. She was commanding us to come out of our hiding place, to come down to the Great Hall.

"Is she out of her mind?" I asked.

"This might be a good moment," Wise Child said. "With Meroot out of the way, at least for now. Do you have the black egg?"

I checked my pocket and nodded. "Are we really going to go?" I said.

"Of course. It will be a chance for the three *dorans* to get together and concentrate their power."

Wise Child was already standing on a chair, lifting the planks that secured us in our prison, and easing herself upward through the hole.

"We must put the planks back and cover them with the carpet. We never know when we might want to use the hiding place again," said Wise Child, as if talking to herself.

It felt strange, and very dangerous, to be in the passage outside Cormac's room, even though, with everyone pressed into service for the feast, it was completely deserted. We scurried down the stairs and along the passages, fearful of what lay in front of us, yet excited, too.

At length we reached the entrance of the hall, passing various footmen coming and going, all too busy to pay us any attention. We sidled into the hall, Wise Child heading for the singer she hoped was Juniper, I making for Euny, who stood leaning against a wall, looking entirely relaxed.

"There you are!" she said. "You've taken your time!"

What happened next was that Euny and the Juniper-lady, who still did not look much like Juniper, drew Wise Child and myself out of the hall and into a little room in the passage beyond it.

"*Are* you Juniper?" I asked the Juniper-lady rather timidly. I was beginning to feel very confused by people changing their identity.

"Yes, I am, Colman," she said firmly, in her old voice. She grinned at me and her eyes sparkled. "Wait till you see me when I am not disguised and then you will know." And she took my hand in a way I found very reassuring.

"First of all," Euny said, "you need to know that Meroot is dead."

"You didn't . . . ," said Juniper, appalled, her voice trailing away.

"Certainly not! I am surprised at you," said Euny.

"*Dorans,* as you know perfectly well, are not in the business of killing."

Juniper accepted the rebuke from her old teacher with a grin. "So what now?" she asked.

"Soon I must go back to the Gray Knight. What the three of us need to do now is concentrate our power so that good may come out of this evil situation and out of this horrible place. Colman, we want your help, too. You are more of a *doran* than you care to know."

"So what do we actually do?" asked Wise Child. "Now, I mean."

Euny glared at her as if she were being exceptionally stupid, though I might easily have asked the same question.

"We become one," she said. "The four of us enter the place where there is no haste, no fear, and no danger, and in entering it together we become as one person. Our powers meld together and the energy is released. It is a force that will overcome evil."

Following Euny's lead, we stood in a circle, held hands, and closed our eyes. There was a pause, and Euny suddenly said, "Now!" just as if we were going to run a race or something. I almost burst out laughing, but then I felt quite irritated because I really had no idea what she was talking about. I did not want to spoil anything for the others, however, all of whom I loved, even Euny.

I tried to sink into a quiet place inside myself. I was holding the hands of Wise Child and Juniper, and then, to my immense surprise, it was suddenly as if some force was circulating through us all, making its way through my body from Wise Child and on to Juniper and thence to Euny. I was wide awake, perhaps more so than usual, but it was a different sort of wakefulness, almost a different place—a place, as Euny had said, beyond haste or fear or danger. Then I knew that I *was* Euny and Wise Child and Juniper and they were me and that between us, if we dared it, was a great power for love and goodness. I heard myself murmuring a prayer for Castle Dore, for Prince Brangwyn, even, to my surprise, for poor wicked Meroot, who had missed the whole point of life and died without finding it. I opened my eyes and smiled at the others.

"Do you think it will work?" Wise Child asked curiously.

"It will suffice," said Euny.

She had scarcely said these words before a sound like thunder echoed through the castle and was thrice repeated. It was not thunder—it was too regular for that—but it was a chilling sound to hear, and we gazed at one another puzzled, trying to think what on earth it could be.

CHAPTER THIRTEEN

The peaceful reverie the three *dorans* and I had enjoyed together was the last moment of calm that would come our way for some time. As we emerged from "the place without haste or fear or danger" and made our way back toward the Great Hall, we found ourselves in a melee of people rushing, or trying to rush, in different directions. Those in the hall, mostly the diners, were trying to get out into the main part of the castle; others, some of them soldiers, were trying to force their way into the hall.

"What on earth's going on?" I heard Wise Child murmur beside me. The four of us were being pushed away from the Great Hall toward the grand staircase that led to the apartments of Meroot and the Gray Knight. Suddenly a silence fell on the whole company—an extraordinary contrast to the hubbub that had preceded it—and looking up, I could see the Gray Knight standing above us at the head of the stairs, quelling the throng by the force of his personality. He was very pale, though his eyes blazed with anger.

"Silence!" he commanded, although already all

conversation had died away. "The castle is surrounded by men who appear to be fully armed. The noise you heard was the sound of a battering ram. Needless to say, it had no effect on our gates. All soldiers must report at once for duty. Caradoc's company are to go to the battlements, where they will prepare to repel invaders. Brychan and his men are to go to the rear of the castle to defend it, in particular against any attempt to enter it by way of the stream. Kinmark and his men are to join me in the Great Hall and from there we will man the front of the castle. I recommend our guests ascend to the private apartments and wait there until the situation becomes clearer. I have instructed the servants to wait upon your wishes."

The knight began to descend the stairs, and a hubbub of conversation broke out. I could hear the guests, in voices near to panic in some cases, wondering who could have attacked the castle, and whether they themselves were in any danger. Euny, I suddenly noticed, had disappeared.

"What do you think we should do?" Wise Child asked Juniper.

"Find a place where we can see a bit of what's going on," said Juniper. "The south tower, perhaps." The south tower was at the front of the castle and looked out on the drawbridge and the front courtyard. From the roof you could see over the drawbridge into the country outside the gates.

It took us a while to escape from the crowd of guests

milling around the stairs, but soon we were making our way up the winding staircase that led to the south tower. There was no sign of any soldiers, and we guessed they were massing on the central battlements, ready to shoot arrows or pour boiling oil on any who attempted to force their way into the castle itself.

At the top of the tower was a roofed enclosure that covered the staircase, and we could comfortably stand or sit in the lee of it and see the front of the castle and the country beyond. We looked eagerly out at the view. Directly in front of the castle was a line of swordsmen wearing Prince Brangwyn's purple and yellow. They disappeared round the side of the building and out of sight, so we guessed the castle was indeed surrounded by them. Behind them stood men wearing black and red—the colors, so Juniper told us, of the north province, which ruled territory between Cornwall and Wales. Back beyond these two lines, forming a great mass of men in both colors, were archers, their yew bows standing tall above them.

"So many!" I gasped. I had never expected that so many would join the men of Castle Dore. In front of his army, riding Golden, was Prince Brangwyn, and beside him was a standard-bearer carrying his flag, which flapped so briskly in the breeze that we could hear the noise that it made.

"May the Mother save him!" I heard Juniper murmur. After a moment she said, "He sits a horse just like my father, who was a famous horseman. He could *be* King Mark."

I thought I saw a tear in her eye.

"He's good at chess, too," put in Wise Child. "Though I beat him sometimes. And he's a good poet."

"The question now," said Juniper, "is, are they going to attack, or are they simply going to besiege the castle, cut off supplies of food, and starve the knight out? If they attack, they risk the loss of many men." Her voice broke a little as she said this, and I knew that it was Brangwyn she was thinking of. It was unbearable to think of losing her brother when she was just about to find him again.

The sun was going down, and I noticed Juniper shivering a little, whether from evening cold or from dread of the fighting to come, I didn't know.

"It doesn't look as if anything will happen tonight," said Wise Child finally. "Surely Brangwyn's army won't stand there all night?"

"I guess they will take it in turns to rest or keep watch," Juniper said. "Luckily, it's a fine night."

"What I can't understand," I said, "is how Prince Brangwyn got here so quickly. I know Golden is a fast horse, but I do not see how he had time to ride to Castle Dore and back again, let alone lead an army on foot."

"It's simple," said Juniper. "Erc sent Nectan to tell us when Brangwyn would escape, and the army of Castle Dore and the Northland marched out to meet him. He had only to turn round and lead them back here. He must have waited until they actually arrived here to discard the cloth of disguise."

"He does not know that Meroot is dead," Wise Child commented. "I wish I could tell him."

"What are *we* going to do?" I could not resist asking. Why was I always the anxious one who worried over the details?

"I think I must reappear among the guests," said Juniper. "The Gray Knight might want me to sing."

"I think we had better try to get back to Cormac's room," Wise Child suggested. "At least we can get some sleep there. I feel much safer now Meroot is no longer able to hurt us."

We arranged a rendezvous with Juniper the next day, and Juniper and Wise Child parted with a hug that showed how much they had missed each other.

When we got to Cormac's room, Cormac was there waiting for us. The Gray Knight had kept him watching by Meroot's body while he went down to make his speech on the staircase. Later, when the knight observed Brangwyn riding at the head of his troops, he had been baffled. He consequently not only made sure that every door was locked, but had put a watch on each one, so that even those with a key to a door could not get out of the castle.

"Does the knight grieve over Meroot?" Wise Child asked Cormac curiously before we slid into our hiding place.

"I think he does. Meroot was a bad person, and the knight is no better—they both chose to practice wicked forms of magic—but I think they loved each other, and he is very distressed. From our point of view that could be a help. His pain distracts him. It makes him less effective as a leader."

We slept briefly and uneasily that night. It was like being near the end of a story and longing to know how things would turn out, only it also felt scarier than even the most exciting story.

The next morning I woke with a worrying feeling that something unpleasant was about to happen, and Wise Child's expression made me feel that she might share my premonition. We set off for our meeting with Juniper. We did not use the great staircase, where we could be stopped, but sidled down a more remote staircase, meaning to make our way back to the Great Hall through the passages used by the servants to bring food from the kitchen. We could not have chosen worse.

"That's them! Stop them!" said a rough voice. Looking up, we saw a soldier, the soldier who had spoken to us the night we had got away from the dungeon. We turned away from him to flee, only to realize that other soldiers waited farther along the passage.

"What'll we do with them?" one of the other soldiers asked after we'd been caught.

"Take them to the knight," the first soldier said. "The

mistress was convinced that they were conspiring with his high and mighty self, *King* Brangwyn. Then they vanished, and got me and my mate into serious trouble. I can't wait to tell the knight that I've found them."

We were marched toward the knight's apartments. It was terrible. Meroot was dead, the confrontation with the men of Castle Dore that might change everything was about to begin, and at this crucial moment we had fallen into the hands of the knight, who might well torture us just as Meroot had been planning to do. Our hearts were very heavy as the soldiers pushed and hurried us up the stairs.

The Gray Knight had obviously not slept at all. He sat slumped in a chair. His eyes were red, either from tired-ness or weeping, and his hair, usually so neat, stood in uncombed tufts around his head. He seemed more alive after the soldier had pushed us forward and told his story, and it occurred to me that if he loved Meroot and thought we had betrayed her, he might treat us all the more harshly. He sent the soldiers curtly back to their posts, leaving us alone with him.

"Do you know what we do with traitors?" he asked ominously. We shook our heads, not really wanting the answer. "We kill them," he said. "As painfully as possible. You may think that because you are children we will spare you. You will be disappointed. We will kill you as an exam-ple to others who betray us."

"Betray you?" Wise Child said bravely, in a voice from

which, I could tell, she was trying to exclude a wobble. "Why do you think we have done that?"

"Do not waste time arguing with me. The mistress told me everything, about your witchcraft and your friendship with Brangwyn. It is obvious now who helped him to escape."

"King Brangwyn has escaped?" said Wise Child in tones of astonishment. The knight turned his cold, weary eyes on her.

"Do not bother to lie to me," he said.

But Wise Child would not be cowed. "The only evidence you have against us—or rather that my lady had—is that she found a flask of purple liquid among our things. I did not know that it was anything special. I thought it was wine. And as I do not like wine much, I had not got round to drinking it."

I must say that Wise Child, usually a very truthful girl, was a very convincing liar. What made me feel she was rather clever, however, had a very different effect on the knight.

I saw a little flame of anger gleam in his eyes, and he stood up and approached menacingly. "Be quiet! You are a wicked child, and you will be punished accordingly."

Wise Child was not one to take insults lying down. "No, I am not," she said, "so don't call me names!"

Some adults might have been impressed at the courage of this young girl, but the knight was not one of them. He swung back his arm and smacked Wise Child across the face. She fell to the floor and cried out in pain.

I don't know quite what seized me. Without even stopping to think, I reached into my pocket, took out the black egg the Mother had given me, and flung it with all my strength at the Gray Knight. The egg broke open upon his chest, leaving a smear of perfectly ordinary-looking yolk.

There was a moment when the knight stood and stared at me with a look of growing astonishment, and then his hand went to his throat and he started to choke. He gasped for breath, and tears began to stream from his eyes. After a minute or two he fell to the floor. In his agony he gestured toward the door, as if supposing that we would call his guards.

"We must get out of here!" Wise Child said. We knew that if we left by the door through which we had entered, we would be seized by the guards. There were two other possibilities. One was the window, but a glance from that told us that it would not help us—there was a sheer drop to the courtyard below. There remained another door, and leaving the knight where he was, we quickly crossed the room and opened it. To our relief it opened upon a staircase, the sort that servants use, and without even discussing it, we shut the door behind us on the knight's struggling body and ran down the stairs as fast as we could.

We had no idea how long we had to escape. Probably the knight's servants and guards were too afraid of him to dare to disobey his orders and interrupt him, but as time went by and nobody emerged from his room, they would begin to wonder and perhaps investigate. We could not risk Juniper's safety by being seen with her, and the thought of returning to the secret room was intolerable to us both.

Wanting to escape and knowing how to do it were two different things, however. We knew that a watch had been placed on all the doors of the castle. There was no question of getting out of any of them unchallenged. I soon realized that the stairs we were using must come out in the yard at the back of the castle, where Wise Child and I had worked so hard in our first days at Caerleon.

"Listen!" I said to Wise Child, so out of breath by now that it was difficult to speak. "I've got an idea! Do you remember, at the Cave of the Mermaids, when Juniper told the outlaws how she and Finbar escaped the castle all those years ago? They used the stream!"

Wise Child, while not ceasing to run downstairs as fast as she could, managed to turn on me a look of warm admiration.

"Yes!" she said. "The only thing is, the Gray Knight stationed soldiers to guard the stream, remember?"

"We must look as if we are doing some necessary chore," I said. "After all, the life of the castle has to go on, even if it is under siege."

It helped that we knew that part of the castle so well. Wise Child and I went to the deserted room where the washing of the castle always lay around in heaps. Together we piled some of it into a basket, and carrying it between us with a scrubbing board laid over the top, we made our way out into the yard.

As we had foreseen, it was full of soldiers. None of them, so far as we could see, were the pair who had recognized us earlier. We heaved a sigh of relief.

They greeted our appearance with jokes. "Going to use the clothes as white flags?" one of them called out.

"It's always important to keep clean," Wise Child returned, and I had to giggle. I had never noticed that she cared much about cleanliness.

We knelt down by the stream as we had often done before, though rather nearer to the archway, where it disappeared into the darkness. We drew up a bucket of water, dipped one of the cloths in it, and began to scrub it on the board to get it clean. For a while the soldiers idly watched us, then one of them started a game of dice, and soon all of them were intent upon it.

"It's now or never," I muttered to Wise Child. Trying to make as little splash as we could, we left the washing on the bank and slipped into the water. I heard Wise Child stifle a gasp. The water was cold! Breathing quickly, we swam into the dark. At one point we had to hold our breath for several yards as we passed under the wall of the castle. There in the dark I suddenly remembered Juniper and Finbar talking about how they had used a black egg on the knight. How strange that we had come to use the very same protection against him.

Then Wise Child and I rose to the surface. She held up the silver moon, and by its dim light we could just see a narrow path running along the right side of the stream. We dragged our dripping bodies out onto the path, and, shivering in the cool air, ran along it to warm ourselves up.

"We must pray," said Wise Child, "that the knight did not have the time to put a sentry at the far end of this path."

This had not occurred to me, and a lump of terror rose in my throat.

"Oh no!" I cried.

"We have not come this far to be defeated by a sentry," Wise Child said stoutly. "It'll be all right, you'll see. Look, the end cannot be far away and the silver moon is not giving out the red light of danger."

It was true. It maintained the dull purple light that told us we were safe. We soon saw why. The lone sentry that the knight, probably remembering Juniper and Finbar, had thought to place at the end of the path lay fast asleep on the bank as we emerged from the tunnel. We tiptoed past him and soon reached the road beyond.

"What now?" I asked.

"Go on until we come upon some of Prince Brangwyn's men. It can't be long. We'll say that we have escaped from Caerleon and want to talk to him. We can give him first-hand information about what is going on inside the castle."

She was silent for a while, and then she said, "I hate having left Juniper behind and not even having said goodbye. She will have no idea what became of us. I hope she will be all right."

I could not think of anything to say to this. I knew Juniper would be distressed when we did not appear.

"Perhaps Euny will find her and help her," I said.

"I wonder what became of Euny after our being together? She seemed to vanish after that."

I began to be aware that I was very tired. I think I may have been feeling shock after the horror of being arrested by the soldiers and bullied by the Gray Knight with the threat of death. Left to myself, I would have lain down in some quiet spot and had a sleep, but Wise Child marched stoutly on, and I did not dare suggest stopping. As if she had heard my thoughts, she said, "It's good to get this part over quickly. We don't know if any of the Gray Knight's men are out scouting on his behalf, and it would be terrible if we fell into their clutches again."

She was right, of course, and I felt ashamed of my earlier thought. And then suddenly we could see a few crude tents ahead of us, and soldiers coming and going from them. We stopped. Yes, they were wearing Prince Brangwyn's colors. Timidly we went forward and gave our rehearsed speech.

"The prince is sleeping, young lady," one of the soldiers said to Wise Child.

"I think the prince would want to see us as soon as possible," she said. "We have come from Caerleon, and we have important information for him."

The soldier went away, and soon came back and told us to follow him. We were heartened to see Golden tethered near the biggest of the tents, and he raised his head as we passed, recognizing us. The prince was sitting up in his tent, trying to fight off sleep, and he regarded us with amazement.

"Wise Child! Colman! Where did you spring from? And what happened to your face?" He was looking at the huge bruise where the knight had struck Wise Child.

Not without some pride, we described our escape to him, going on to tell him about the throwing of the black egg at the Gray Knight and the state to which it had reduced him.

"This could make a big difference," he said.

"And Meroot is dead," I said.

"Yes, I knew that."

"How?" I asked, amazed.

"Juliot told me," he said. "She is here, by the way, and she explained a lot of things to me that I had not quite understood."

We did not even bother to ask how Euny had got herself there. We had learned that she was a law unto herself.

"Tell us about your own escape," Wise Child said.

"It was lovely," said the prince simply. "I enjoyed every moment of it. Golden ran as he has never run before, as if he knew how important it was.

"Soon I had outstripped everyone else in the race, and then, halfway back to Castle Dore, I met all the Castle Dore men, along with their allies from the Northland. They recognized Golden and knew about the cloth of disguise, so I was able to maintain the ruse until we arrived at Caerleon itself, to give Cormac as much time as possible. I cannot tell you the joy at seeing my people, and it was all your doing. I could never have done it, never even have dared to do it, without you. Now, whatever happens, I shall never let myself fall again into the clutches of Caerleon. I would rather die ascending the battlements."

"What does Euny—sorry, Juliot—think should happen next?" Wise Child asked curiously.

"She thinks we should hold the siege and gradually starve them out."

"I would think that, except that Juniper is there," said Wise Child gravely. "Your sister, my teacher, and Juliot's pupil," she explained to the prince.

The prince nodded. "It may be that now the knight has been struck down, they will lose their resolution. How long will he remain sick?"

"It will be months before he is fully recovered, and to his men it may seem that he will never recover," said Wise Child. "At present he will be unconscious quite a lot of the time, with intervals when he will talk wildly and appear unlike himself."

"Good!" said the prince. "Couldn't be better, from our point of view. Somehow, I cannot spare any sympathy for him. He and Meroot treated the people of Castle Dore abominably. Not only them. The rumor is that many of his own people are coming to join us. He and Meroot taxed them unmercifully and stole some of their farms, with brutal punishments and killings for any who resisted." He paused. "I must get up now. There is much to do. You must both have a rest and some breakfast."

"Just a quick nap," said Wise Child typically. "I don't want to miss anything."

"Sleep while you can," said the prince. "The next act may be a slow one." He was up now, partly dressed from when he went to bed, bathing his face and hands in rosewater, strapping on his breastplate and sword, obviously eager to get back to his men. Before he did so, however, he held out his arms to Wise Child and hugged her.

"Ouch!" she said. "That breastplate hurts!"

"Sorry," the prince replied. "Didn't think of that!" And then, smiling at me, he hugged me, too. She was quite right. It did hurt, but I said nothing. "You see?" he said to Wise Child. "Colman is made of tougher metal."

"Huh!" she said.

Mid-morning, refreshed by breakfast, a wash, and a brief sleep, Wise Child and I made our way toward the front of the castle, passing many of Brangwyn's troops and followers on the way, who had camped and were tethering horses in the wooded area to the east of the castle.

"There are a lot of them," Wise Child said. "The Northland must have turned out in force."

Neither of us was prepared for the sight that met our eyes when we reached the front aspect of the castle. On that huge plain there were men as far as the eye could see. There were men with bows, men with spears, men on horseback, men with battering rams and metal hooks for scaling castle walls. We suddenly understood that we were looking at the uprising of most of the men of Cornwall—those who lived locally and had suffered badly under Meroot and the Gray Knight; those, like the people of Castle Dore, who had endured miserable subjugation; those from the north, who knew Caerleon merely as a dangerous neighbor who would have to be confronted sooner or later; and probably those from farther afield, who also dreaded the knight's military power.

"Do you think it was the power of the *dorans* that brought them?" I asked Wise Child.

"That, and the pride and wickedness of Meroot and the knight, which made them many enemies. And the courage of Prince Brangwyn in breaking out of Caerleon."

"And the courage of Wise Child in going to Caerleon and encouraging him to do so," I said.

Wise Child smiled. "Maybe. Good things, unexpected things, happen when people who love good take risks and work together. I wish something would happen, though. All this hanging about makes me nervous."

Almost as if those within the castle had heard her words, the drawbridge of the castle came down and a man dressed in the colors of the Gray Knight emerged from the entrance, carrying a white flag, which he waved nervously in the direction of the prince, who, a strong, handsome presence, was mounted on Golden. The prince beckoned him forward and they talked together. Then the knight's man turned and went back into the castle.

The prince signaled to some of his captains, who came and conferred with him. They then rode off in various directions across the huge field, pausing, we could see, to converse with different groups of men.

"Oh, I do want to know what is going on!" Wise Child groaned.

Presently the herald from Caerleon emerged again, this time accompanied by the Gray Knight's captains. After the last of them had emerged, there came a group of four men carrying a stretcher, and on the stretcher, we could guess even from a distance, lay the Gray Knight. He lay motionless. They placed him on the ground in front of the prince.

"I bet Prince Brangwyn asked for him as a hostage," I said. "So that if his own men enter the castle, they will be quite safe."

Prince Brangwyn's men, and later the prince himself, did enter the castle. On his explicit instructions, no one in the castle was harmed, and the women and children were treated with the utmost kindness and courtesy. A treaty was signed by the knight's lieutenant, by Prince Brangwyn, by Keyne, the leader of the Northland, and by the *reguli* of other groups who had now become their allies. It left Caerleon in no doubt that if it took arms against any of them, all these others would rise up to attack them. The unhappy days when Caerleon ruled the southwest by terror were over.

A few weeks later, with various repayments agreed for the damage done to Castle Dore, together with restorations of grain and cattle, we all returned to Castle Dore. The prince gave immediate instructions that the Wooden Palace was to be rebuilt with even greater splendor than it had enjoyed in his father's day, and he said that he would be crowned there as soon as it was complete. Freed of their crushing burden of paying tribute to Caerleon, the people, we knew, would soon recover their original prosperity. The prince gave a great feast for all his people, at which we drank the magnificent wine Caerleon had given us as part of their reparation and ate ox roasted on the green where Perquin had once lorded over us. The prince made a speech, and then we all joyfully drank and ate and danced until the sun went down and the people of Castle Dore, happy and content, made their way to their own homes.

Back in the royal apartments, those of us who had worked and plotted for just such an outcome were silent at first. We were tired after all the exertions of the day, and the prince's speech had expressed our feelings about the present. He and Juniper, delighted at having found each other again, often exchanged glances or took hands. They would sit in corners together having long conversations, each of them catching up on details of the other's life. He had plans to build her a house close to Castle Dore, but in the meantime was delighted to have her living with him. Wise Child and Juniper also often embraced each other, glad that all the recent dangers were passed. No one could have foreseen, when we left Dalriada, the adventures ahead of us. Cormac and Finbar, who had both done so much to help, rejoiced in our happiness. And Euny? She seemed totally unsurprised by everything that had happened. When Prince Brangwyn offered to build her a house, just as his father King Mark had done before him, she shook her head and announced that she intended to return to the site of her old hut in the Outlands and rebuild it.

"But perhaps," Juniper said gently, "you would let the prince give you some wood, and let some of his men travel with you to do the rebuilding?"

Euny wrestled with this, obviously tempted by the offer but unwilling as ever to appear gracious and grateful.

"Oh, I suppose so," she said at last. "Though I would probably do it better myself." She paused. "There is another bit of business that we *dorans* need to do," she went on. "I think with the four of us, we can manage it. Yes, Colman, I am including you. One day you will be a proper *doran,* I think, and Wise Child, too, though you both have much training ahead of you. Cormac, would you mind coming here a moment?"

The four of us stood in a ring around Cormac, for what purpose I had not the least idea. We held hands, exactly as we had done amid the terrors of Caerleon, and I closed my eyes, wondering what on earth was supposed to happen. If I needed to concentrate, it would be good to know what I was being asked to think about. I tried to empty my mind of the usual nonsense that filled it and get myself into the place "beyond haste or fear or danger." Suddenly I was very aware of the warm hand of Wise Child on one side of me and of Juniper on the other, and of a current or tide passing through me and making its way round the circle. A thought, or rather a picture, entered the space I had made in my head. It was a picture of Cormac, strong and handsome, without the mutilated nose, the twisted mouth, and the deep scarring all over his face that spoiled his appearance. I could hear Euny and Juniper murmuring words that I could not understand, and without knowing what they said, I consented to their will. Then I opened my eyes, and there, standing in front of me, was a man I knew and did not know—Cormac, with his face transformed.

ABOUT THE AUTHOR

Monica Furlong is best known in the United States for her two award-winning books for young adults, *Wise Child* and its prequel, *Juniper*. In her homeland of England, she was many things—journalist, biographer, novelist, feminist, activist, and social commentator and critic. To all of these roles she brought her abiding commitment to the Christian faith and her simultaneous disillusionment with established social structures. Confronting injustice and hypocrisy wherever she found it, she campaigned for changes to laws that discriminated against homosexuals and successfully led a movement for the ordination of women in the Church of England.

Monica Furlong finished *Colman*, the sequel to *Wise Child*, just before her death in January 2003, in Devon, England. She was seventy-two years old.

COLMAN'S COUSIN . . .

In a remote Scottish village, nine-year-old Wise Child is abandoned by her parents and taken in by Juniper, a healer and sorceress. Under Juniper's kind but stern tutelage, Wise Child learns reading, herbal lore, and even the beginnings of magic. Then Wise Child's mother, the black witch Maeve, reappears. Forced to choose between Maeve and Juniper, Wise Child discovers both her growing supernatural powers and her true loyalties.

"Tightly written . . . mesmerizing and suspenseful."
—*Newsday*

"Exciting, well-written fantasy."
—*Publishers Weekly*

"Rich in detail, high in excitement,
and filled with unforgettable characters."
—*Booklist*

WHEN THE WISE WOMAN
WAS JUST A GIRL . . .

The only child of the king of Cornwall, Juniper enjoys the easy life of a medieval princess. Still, something compels her to leave the palace to study with her godmother, Euny, a harsh but wise woman who teaches the girl about herbs, healing, and the magic within nature. As her training comes to an end, Juniper discovers that her power-hungry aunt is using black magic in an attempt to seize the throne. Armed only with her new, untested powers, Juniper must find a way to stop her—before the kingdom itself is destroyed!

"Fantasy of the caliber of Bradley's *The Mists of Avalon,* and just as satisfying." —*School Library Journal*

"Full of strong, resourceful, wise women. Furlong is a profound and disturbing author who sheds light on our lingering darkness and speaks for tolerance in an intolerant world." —*The Times* (London)